WITH THIS FOREVER

Windswept Bay, Book Ten

DEBRA CLOPTON

With This Forever

He's a risk taker; she's never taken a risk in her life…now she'll risk everything to win his heart.

Seamstress Sammy Jo Lovely has never done a risky thing in her entire life. Now, alone and with a promise to her beloved granny that she'll actually do the things on her bucket list, she's moved to Windswept Bay to change her life. Learning to scuba dive is on top of her list, along with swimming in the ocean, taking a boat ride, and feeling the sand between her toes. Yes, her life has been sheltered. Maybe being near the ocean and a dive shop will inspire her to actually do something. Then she meets her handsome new neighbor and what she wants in life takes on a whole new meaning.

Adventure lover and dive shop owner, Jake Sinclair isn't sure why his quiet, slightly klutzy new neighbor has opened her "Lovely You" women's boutique next door to his dive shop. It's a very unlikely combination—just like they are. But, when he catches sight of her bucket list, he's intrigued and can't help but offer to help her check a few things off…such as "kissing on a moonlit beach." But when it comes to "falling in love," he might be increasingly drawn to everything about Sammy "So" Lovely, but that might be one thing on her list he can't help her check off.

On the romantic shores of Windswept Bay, can Sammy Jo help Jake realize that opening up to love is a risk worth taking?

CHAPTER ONE

Jake Sinclair rammed a hand through his hair as he watched the last of the dive group headed off the dock and walk toward the back entrance of his dive shop. His eyes narrowed when the tall blonde with an attitude turned back and drilled him with fierce, angry eyes. She'd been part of a three-party group mixed in with the other seven-party group. And she'd been trouble from the moment she'd set foot on his boat.

Hoping she'd leave, he turned away and knelt down to double-check that the boat was secured to the dock correctly. He knew it was secured just fine but checking it gave him a reason to look away and let Brandy stomp her way off the dock and off the premises.

Rapid steps on the pier told him no such luck, she was coming back. He braced himself for another unpleasant encounter and shot a glance over his shoulder. A little too late as she shoved him in the back and sent him off the pier. He splashed into the bay and hit the water on his side, did a quick flip and came up fast. A few years as a Navy SEAL, and more years as a dive master, kept him quick in the water. Obviously not as quick as he should be out of the water.

"Okay, that does it—you've got a problem, lady?" he called, spitting mad and tired of ignoring her ridiculous actions in hopes she'd just leave.

She glared down at him with her hands gripping her slender hips. "You ignored me. Nobody does that. And that's what you get. I'm the best thing that could have happened to you."

"Honey, for some reason I'm pretty sure that isn't true."

"Don't call me honey. You lost your chance at

that." She hiked her nose in the air then stormed down the pier like the Tasmanian Devil in a string bikini.

He'd done everything possible to be nice to her without taking her up on her over-the-top advances. He'd finally had to point-blank tell her that he was thirty-two years old and she was nineteen and he wasn't interested. Not to mention she was also not a nice person. And just being sexy wasn't cutting it these days for Jake.

"Come on," she snapped at her friends, who were waiting for her.

They'd obviously had enough and both shook their heads.

"That was not nice, and uncalled for," the nicest of the three, Diana, said. "I'll get my own ride back home."

Good for her. The other girl gave Diana and then him a regretful look before she followed Brandy across the lot. *At least Diana had some sense.*

He swam to the back of the boat.

"That was intense," Caleb, his dive assistant, said as Jake climbed out of the water onto the platform.

"Pretty ridiculous is what I call it." He yanked his shirt off and tossed it to the floor of the boat. "I pity the dude who gets tangled up with that one."

He did not do drama. He enjoyed dating, maybe a little too much. He enjoyed spending time with intriguing women. But nothing about Brandy had intrigued him. She'd been spoiled and mean-spirited from the moment she'd climbed onto his boat. And for some strange reason, she'd thought she could impress him with her bad-mannered moves. He'd dodged her from instant one.

It had been the longest, four-hour round-trip dive excursion he'd ever been on and he'd been thankful they hadn't paid for a five-hour trip. He would have had to call it quits and brought them in early.

Caleb chuckled. "Yeah, that was one scary chick right there."

"Tell me about it." He scowled. "Please tell me I didn't do anything to make her think I was in to her or—"

"Are you kidding?" Caleb broke him off before he could voice any more of his concern that he'd led her on somehow. "You didn't do anything. Diana said she's done this before with guys. She said Brandy spotted you at Paradise Grill one night and has been watching you."

"Watching me?" He raked a hand through his short, wet hair.

"She's got pictures of you on her phone, like she's been trailing you or something."

"Yay for me," Jake muttered. Just what he needed—a college-aged stalker. "I'm sure she's deleting those photos now. Probably burning her phone. Maybe you need to head into the shop and make sure Miss Sunshine isn't causing any trouble inside her car."

"Sure thing." Caleb glanced toward the brunette who hadn't gone with her friends.

"I might see if Diana needs a ride home."

"Yeah, she probably needs it. Tell Fran to lock up the front and I'll take care of the back."

Fran worked the shop while he and his other dive master took the daily dive trips. Jake watched Caleb and Diana head toward the shop, then he turned back to the boat with a sense of relief. Tension eased from his shoulders as he headed into the cabin and pulled a bottle of water from the cooler. He downed the whole thing in less than thirty seconds then he went back up on deck, ready to chill out for a moment. Movement out of the corner of his eye caught his attention and he glanced toward land, half expecting to see blondezilla storming his way again. Instead, he saw a tall, dark-headed woman at the door of the vacant shop connected to his dive shop.

She was stunning, really stunning. He lost all train of thought for a moment as he took her in. She wore a flowing yellow dress that fluttered in the breeze from the bay. As he stared, she turned and caught him looking. Their eyes collided and he froze to the spot.

Who was she?

She headed toward the faded blue van backed into the parking space with its back doors open. Jake watched her load her arms with boxes. She could barely see around the armload but started back to the shop. *There was no way she could see where she was going.* He saw her veer to the left then to the right and he wanted to yell out for her to watch her step, but he didn't. He just held his breath and to his surprise, she made it inside the building without breaking her neck.

Who was she?

His landlord hadn't said anything about someone renting the shop. He would've thought Mrs. Louis would have told him if she'd decided to rent out the space.

The woman reappeared and went back to the van. When she started stacking more boxes in her arms, he decided he needed to go offer to help her. She had started back toward the building as he hopped from the boat. No sooner had he started her way than she went down like a brick wall.

He was already moving, racing down the pier to help her.

Sammy Jo Lovely yelped as she slammed to the ground and face-planted in the middle of the stack of newly sewn, custom skirts she'd been carrying. She managed to turn her hands to try to break her fall but she could tell from the stinging pain that she'd skinned a knee.

She let the impact of the fall settle over her with a groan then rolled to her back and stared up at the picturesque blue sky above her. Of course, the first thought was to wonder if anyone had witnessed her do this clumsy face-plant.

Groaning again, she struggled to sit up.

"Wait," someone yelled. "Don't move."

She looked toward the docks to see the gorgeous, shirtless guy from the boat at the pier who she'd been distracted by moments before her fall. He put both hands on the railing separating the dock from the grassy expanse between them and vaulted effortlessly over the railing and charged her way. *All muscled, tanned, overwhelming inch of him.*

She froze and just watched him cross to her. Seconds later, he knelt by her side and she was blinking at him like an owl at daybreak. Her mouth fell open and she clamped it shut.

"You're hurt. And bleeding," he said, seeing her palms. "Let me help you."

"I'm fine," she managed. Her heart raced. He was so distracting that momentarily she was feeling no pain at all.

"I hate to be the bearer of bad news, but you're not okay." His deep blue eyes were compassionate as he looked at her then her palms and then down toward her knees.

She sighed. "You might be right. I should have been watching where I was going."

"You did have your arms full." He gently helped her sit up by slipping an arm beneath her shoulders and easing her up.

"Great. I was hoping no one saw my act of graceful tumbling." It was one thing to fall flat on her face and no one see her do it. It was an altogether complete other solar system of embarrassing knowing he'd seen the whole thing. Pain was now radiating from her knee and her palms. She bit her lip and tried to ignore it.

"It doesn't matter. You're hurting."

"Just my knee mostly. I'm afraid to look." She gave a shaky laugh. "I'm kind of a chicken when it comes to blood."

"Then don't look. I'll get you inside and take care of it for you."

"No, I can make it—" Her words turned into a gasp when he stood and scooped her into his arms. "Oh, I wasn't expecting you to carry me."

"Well, I am. Do you have water in there?"

"Yes, but this is a bit awkward." Very awkward, actually, to find herself held against his very strong chest with his arms hooked under her knees and her back. She felt breathless looking into his blue, blue eyes.

He cocked his head to the side and winked at her. "I'm Jake Sinclair. I own the dive shop next door. Knowing my name hopefully makes it less awkward. Now, who are you?"

She blinked, trying to look away but could not make herself do so. "Sammy Jo Lovely, otherwise known from here on out as Miss Not-So-Graceful."

He entered the back door. "You're being too hard on yourself. It's nice to meet you, Sammy Jo Lovely."

She gulped hard as he stared into her eyes while

striding, oh so capably, across the room to the chair next to the wall. She hadn't been able to walk two feet carrying a few boxes without falling flat on her face and he was carrying her not-so-light-body, *and* staring into her eyes at the same time. She fought the urge to let her injured hands rest on his impressive, bare-naked chest.

Thankfully he made it to the chair and gently set her in it, then straightened and looked around. "Now point me in the direction of water and a clean cloth and I'll take care of your wounds."

She tried to keep her act together considering he was seemingly unaffected by her not-so-impressive charms. "In there." She pointed toward the bathroom.

He gave her a devastating smile that kicked her insides into a frenzy and she could only imagine had caused much more sophisticated women than herself to lose their hearts, and maybe their heads over him. She had just witnessed the beautiful blonde storm down the pier and shove him into the water. Maybe that had been what had happened to her. Just lost her head over the dark-haired, gorgeous man.

She'd been startled when she'd looked out at the newly arrived boat and witnessed what the woman did. And it had been easy for her to think the guy must have deserved what he'd gotten. But now, she wondered how *anyone* could be mad at him. He was amazing.

He came from the restroom carrying a damp cloth.

"You're really going above and beyond what you need to do. I can take it from here."

He knelt, took one of her hands, and gently lay the cool wet cloth against the scraped skin. "I hope I'm not the only person who would help out in a situation like this. Sorry if that burns." He took her other hand and lightly pressed it with the wet cloth between both palms. His touch was easy and sent her pulse speeding as he smiled at her. "Hold them together and let the coolness of the rag seep in. I'm going to look at your knee, if that's okay with you?"

Her granny would call him a sweetheart and she had to agree. "I hate to admit it but that would probably be best."

Very carefully, he pressed both her palms together

on the cloth. "How is that?"

"It stings, but is feeling better. They aren't too bad, just a few minor scrapes. You're a very nice person. I wasn't expecting that after I saw that pretty blonde woman shove you into the water." The moment the words burst from her lips she gasped.

His eyes swung to hers and suddenly she wished with all her heart she had kept her thoughts to herself.

Why had she even said that?

CHAPTER TWO

"**I** mean, well, she looked like she was getting you back for something."

She was cute. Jake smiled at her turning pink. She was looking at him as if she thought he might toss her into the bay. "I promise, I didn't do anything to her. The lady just has problems, evidently, if she doesn't get her way. And she didn't get her way today."

"I'm sorry, none of my business. I don't even know why I said anything. It just came out."

"It's okay. Let's tend to this knee. And the blonde, well, she booked a dive trip and then used the whole four hours to abuse her friends and try to impress me. But meanness isn't something I'm impressed with. I'll be right back. Don't go anywhere. I'm going to jog over to my store and get some first aid supplies."

"Thank you. I really hate that I'm being so much trouble."

"Not a problem. At least you aren't pushing me into the bay," he called over his shoulder and headed out the door.

His thoughts stuck on her smile as he jogged next door, where he had a large first aid cabinet and several first aid kits to keep around and on the boats. He grabbed a kit, checked it to make sure it had what he needed and then he headed back to Sammy Jo Lovely. He smiled at her name. It fit. She was lovely. And she was about as different from the blondezilla he'd been unimpressed by as could be.

His new neighbor had his attention.

He grabbed a bottle of water from the refrigerator in case she needed a drink, and then he hurried back to her. Her pretty creations were still scattered across the pavement, so he set the water and first aid kit down and quickly gathered up the colorful stacks of skirts and put them back in the box. The material was soft and silky and made him think of their creator. She seemed gentle, soft-spoken, and her hair was as silky as the cloth.

Beside the stack was an open notebook. He grabbed that, too, and then he picked up the first aid kit and water and went inside the shop. He caught her just as she lifted the rag and peeked at her knee. Her mouth dropped open and her eyes scrunched closed as she slapped the rag back down to cover it up.

"I told you not to look." He set the armload on the counter. The notebook slipped from the stack and fell to the counter.

She looked pained. "I know. I'm a grown woman and I can't deal with a little blood. I hate being a wimp but I am. I feel guilty imposing on you. Thank you for picking those up."

"You're welcome and don't feel guilty." He noticed the notebook had a list written on it. His gaze caught on the title of the open page. *My Bucket List* was written across the top.

His gaze scanned the list:

Open my business.

Feel sand between my toes.

Swim in the ocean.

Scuba dive—if can get up the nerve.

Ride in a boat.

Kiss a man on a romantic, moonlit beach.

Fall in love.

There were a few more items on the list, but his gaze snagged on *Kiss a man on a romantic, moonlit beach.* His curiosity was most definitely piqued.

He strode across the room, his mind churning. *Had his new neighbor never been kissed? Or just never been kissed on a moonlit beach?*

He could not believe she'd never kissed a man, so it just had to be the moonlit beach.

Twisting the cap off the water he knelt and handed it to her. Their fingers brushed and tingles of hot electric impulses raced through him.

She froze and didn't draw the bottle away immediately. Their fingers continued to touch. Her eyes had widened. "Um, thank you," she said after a second and took the bottle. "But really, I can doctor my own knee."

Electricity buzzed through him even after they weren't touching and he couldn't look away as she tilted the water up and took a drink.

Never been kissed. The thought echoed through him again. *No way.*

No, *no* way that could be true. He told himself to cut it out and concentrate.

"I'll bandage it. I don't mind. You just relax and drink your water. When I caught you peeking at your knee a second ago, you looked a little green."

Two lines formed between her pretty eyes. "It's a curse. I feel helpless. It just seems wrong."

"If it makes you feel any better, I'm trained in first aid from my days as a Navy SEAL, so I promise you that I won't faint on the job." He winked.

"You were a SEAL? I should have guessed. You looked like Superman jumping that railing earlier."

He chuckled. "Those skills still come in handy. Now, relax. I can deal with this." He removed the rag from her knee. "This will sting. But it needs to be done. And you're going to have some stiffness for a week but hopefully not longer."

"I can handle a little pain. I just get queasy looking at wounds."

He applied the antiseptic and though she tensed, she didn't make a sound.

"I'm sorry it's hurting you."

"It's fine, says wimpy me to the Navy SEAL." She frowned. "I really do feel like a total mess now that I know what an amazing tough guy you are."

He laughed. "How do you know that?"

"I've watched those reports on what you have to go through to get the title of Navy SEAL. I don't swim in the ocean. I don't have a pain tolerance. I don't have a bone of adventure in my entire body. So that's just a few of the reasons. You know good and well that you're a tough guy."

He chuckled, enjoying the sound of her voice. "People can do far more than they think they can. Especially in extraordinary situations. Why don't you swim in the ocean?" *Why haven't you ever kissed a man?*

She chuckled. "Boy, you switch subjects fast."

"I'm interested in learning about you. I already know about myself."

She smiled. "Fine. I just haven't. My life has been complicated. My knee is looking better," she said in an obvious attempt of her own to change the subject.

"Trying to use my tactic isn't fair. Why don't you swim in the ocean? Why are you not adventurous? Are you afraid?"

She inhaled and her gaze moved away from his. "Like I said, my life has been complicated and well, no opportunity. I'm a wimp on so many levels—it's ridiculous but true. However, I have a plan to change that."

He applied salve to her knee. She knit her brow together over her pretty emerald eyes and took a breath. He finished bandaging the knee then met her gaze directly. "What kind of plan?" He smoothed the edges of the bandage. Her skin was soft and he focused on what she'd said rather than the feel of her skin. *Or that she'd never kissed a man.* Or *might* never have been kissed, he reminded himself. Still, the possibility was just unbelievable if it were true.

"I have a list of things I'm going to do. I'm not going to stop until everything is checked off. Moving here was number one on my list and I'm here."

"A bucket list?" *Man, she intrigued him.* Her cheeks tinged slightly and he wasn't sure whether he should tell her he'd seen the list. He didn't feel right pretending he hadn't seen it.

"Actually, yes." She blushed. "Not a big one. Just a small one. Right now."

She was adorable. "Okay, I need to come clean. I saw part of the list when I picked your notebook up outside."

Her pink went to red. "You saw that?"

He nodded, enjoying how beautiful she was. "I just caught a glimpse of it before I shut it."

"I guess you saw that I haven't ever really had the opportunity to do much. Adventure is *not* my middle name."

He thought about the kissing part and still couldn't figure that one out. "So, you want to scuba dive?" He gave her an encouraging smile. "If you're looking for adventure, you've moved into the right neighborhood. I'll be glad to help you out on any adventure you want. I'm actually a bit of an adventure nut."

They stared at each other. He was still thinking about the kissing part—he was obsessed with the kissing part. Especially when her gaze dropped to his lips. Suddenly he wondered whether she was thinking about kissing, too. The room suddenly felt a lot warmer.

"I'm talking myself into the scuba dive. It's not that easy," She looked down at her knee. "Well, yay, my knee looks better."

"Yes, it does, and my new neighbor is avoiding the question. Thankfully your knee isn't as bad as I first thought. But it will still take it a few days before it starts getting better. You never said what this store is?"

A smiled touched her lips. "It's a boutique of unique items for women that I have shipped in from around the world. I also design my own line of clothing and scarves. I have an online business but this is going to be my first official storefront. I'm venturing out."

"Well, you moved into the right neighborhood. I have four sisters, a mom, and four sisters-in-law. I'll be sure to spread the word."

"Wow. You have a huge family."

"Yes, I do. And you chose to put a women's boutique next door to a dive shop? Interesting choice of locations. But with my family spreading the word, it shouldn't matter too much where your shop is."

"That would be wonderful. And as for this building it was the right price. And it comes with that small apartment above."

His antenna went up. "You mean those two rooms and that closet called a bathroom? You're moving in?"

"Yes. And it's big enough for me. And convenient to the business and it has that cute little balcony too. I can see myself sitting out there in the evenings while I work. The building just makes sense. Thank you so much for helping me."

"It does have a good view of the marina and Windswept Bay. I live down the road, so if you ever need anything, I'll be near."

She laughed. "I promise I am not going to be the neighbor who bugs you all the time. And I do not plan on falling again, so you're officially off the hook. Speaking of which, I'm all better now and I know you have things to do. I can manage from here on out." She placed her feet on the ground and carefully stood.

He stood also. Wanting to know more about her and not at all ready to leave her. "But your hands? I need to bandage them."

"They're fine, just barely scratched. Thanks for everything."

He frowned. "I don't mind."

She looked tempted then shook her head. "I'm fine. Really."

"Is there anything else I can do? I hate to leave you—"

She chuckled. "*I'm fine*. See, I can walk and everything. I need to change these clothes and I'll be able to get back to work. I'm moving a little slower than before, but I'll make it."

He checked the time on his watch. He was

supposed to meet Grant and Gage, his brothers-in-law, at the reef in thirty minutes for a dive they were doing for some shots Grant wanted to paint. Grant was a famous sea life painter and was meeting him there in his own boat. He thought about calling Grant and cancelling. He didn't want to leave. "If you're sure," he said, reluctantly. "Then I'll go. But, be careful out there."

Her eyes twinkled. "I promise to watch my steps."

He had a hard time making himself move. "I'll leave that kit there for you just in case. I have them by the dozens next door. If you need anything, call 911. My brother Levi is chief of police and my brother-in-law Ryan is a deputy. They'll take care of you."

She frowned. "Jake, I'm not going to need to do that. I'm fine. But thanks for the information."

He heard a hint of irritation in her tone and berated himself for suddenly turning into a mother hen. "Sorry, I didn't mean to make it sound like you were automatically going to need help. Okay, I'll go now. I am only digging myself deeper into this hole. I'll drop by tomorrow and see how it's going. If you need anything heavy lifted, I don't mind helping. Remember that."

"I'll remember. Thanks again."

He moved and wondered what was wrong with him. He'd seen smiles before and black hair. He'd even seen twinkling green eyes and soft, pearl-toned skin. And pink lips made for kissing. *Kissing.*

Whew, he could not get kissing off his mind. He was obsessed. He frowned and backed away, not sure why he was so infatuated with Sammy Jo Lovely. But he was.

Her eyes met his and his pulse raced like a rocket-fueled speedboat. Yep, it wasn't rocket science—it was pure chemistry.

He wanted to help Sammy Jo with her bucket list.

Especially the never-been-kissed part.

CHAPTER THREE

Sammy Jo carried the last box of skirts and camisoles from the van and set the stack on the shelf. Her knee was throbbing and she sat down for just a moment. She couldn't stop thinking about her knight-in-shining-armor-of-a-new-neighbor.   The man…took her breath away.

And he knew she had a bucket list. Just a little embarrassing.

Make that a lot embarrassing.

She pushed thoughts of him away and went back to work. She pulled the large bag containing her blow-up bed out of her van and limped up the stairs to her apartment. She focused on each step and took her time because the last thing she wanted to do was fall and need to call 911. That would be awful if Jake's brother or brother-in-law had to come rescue her right after Jake.

That would certainly set in stone a total klutz had just moved next door to him. Especially because she was sure that Jake Sinclair had never had a clumsy moment in his life. She paused on the step and stared at the railing he had vaulted over like a ninja. The man had been wonderful. Amazing. Spectacular—

Enough!

No more thinking about him.

She was here to make her dreams a reality. This building held her dreams. It was small and kind of ugly, but when she got through decorating it was going to be fantastic. It wasn't in the best spot but it would work. The fact that it had the dive shop right next door had been almost like a sign to her when she'd found the place. She'd come here hoping…no, determined to change her way of life, to widen her horizons. The dive shop was like an everyday reminder that adventure awaited her. Going on a dive was on her bucket list—but it was a huge stretch because she was claustrophobic. The thought of being underwater sent her into a panic. But if she could do that, she could do anything. So she would dream.

The picturesque small community of Windswept Bay had so much to offer her. Not only did it have a flood of tourists all year long who would appreciate her specialty designs, it was beautiful, quaint, and with plenty of exciting things to do. Surely here she could live a little.

It was truly a lovely place and her grandmother's most favorite memory. She had come because her sweet gram had told her this was where she should start her new life.

And the beautiful tourist town was the perfect place to open the first physical store of her Lovely You Designs. Thinking about her grandmother made her smile a bittersweet smile. Her heart ached, she missed her so much. It had only been four months since she'd passed away but despite that, Sammy Jo had worked hard to make the move happen.

Her grandmother would be so proud of her and she wanted this for Sammy Jo. She had come up with the name of her designs. Gram had always wanted more for Sammy Jo and had hated that Sammy Jo had put her life on hold to take care of her and her granddaddy. Because of Gram's dreams for her, Sammy Jo stood here now, about to make both their dreams come true.

She stared at the moonlight from the window and sighed. She was here. She'd taken the first step in changing her life. And tomorrow she'd take more steps.

"I'm doing it, Gram," she whispered, gazing up at the moon. Loneliness seeped in around her. She breathed in deep and let the air out slowly. *She was doing it.* And it might be one step at a time, but they would be forward. "They'll be good steps, Gram. I promise."

She sighed and closed her eyes.

By morning, she was all the more determined to get things rolling. She managed to change her bandage without actually looking at the knee. She'd done a lot of squinting and heavy breathing. Then she'd headed down the stairs to get her day going. She paused midway down to admire the way the morning sunlight sparkled on the topaz water. Windswept Bay was gorgeous. She felt energized by the sounds of the surf. She couldn't believe she was really here.

Her phone rang and she fished the cell from her purse. Her friend Roxie's photo showed on the screen. As she answered the call, her gaze snagged on Jake on his boat. Oh goodness, the man took her breath away.

She could absolutely stare at him all day. It was very nearly obsessive as she watched him moving about the boat, checking things and just standing for a moment with his hands on his hips, staring out over the bay. The bay was all the more fantastic with him in the view.

"Good morning," she said, completely distracted as she sank onto the steps to talk and enjoy the wonderful view. She was only human, after all.

"Hey girly-girl. Is it as beautiful as it looks online? Is it as great as Gram said it would be?"

She laughed at Roxie's bright voice. "Um, yes. It truly *is* as beautiful as Gram remembered it."

"Yes! I am so glad I gave you a kick in the pants to follow your dreams. Your gram, God rest her soul, adored Windswept Bay. I know she's smiling knowing you're there. Have you checked out the dive shop yet? Booked a dive?"

Sammy Jo laughed. "I just got here. I've barely unloaded the van. But I did meet the owner of the dive shop." She smiled as she watched him answer his own phone. He stood on the end of the boat with his back to her as he looked out at the bay.

"Is Mr. Adventure as handsome up close as he is on the website?"

They had checked Jake's business out online and though she had felt flutters of attraction looking at his smiling face on his website, it did not do the man justice. She thought of his compassionate blue eyes and his strong, bare chest—the one hidden by a red T-shirt at the moment. She pushed the bare chest out of her mind. But it was a strong memory and kept fighting its way back into the picture. "Yes, the picture was accurate. Actually, he's better-looking in person and super sweet."

"*Sweet.* Do I hear interest in your voice? How did you meet him?"

"He, um, helped me get moved in," she squeaked and fought down the voices screaming in the background that yes, she was very definitely interested.

"Wonderful. How'd that happen?"

She frowned. "Honestly, we met when I face-planted on the pavement and he came to my rescue."

There was a moment of silence. "Seriously? Are you okay?"

"I'm fine. My knee and my pride are scraped up but I'm fine. He was on his boat and saw me hit the pavement and came running. The man vaulted a fence to get to me." She was still amazed by that.

"I'm impressed. You like him? Maybe he'll help you get a few things off your list and not just the scuba diving. Like being kissed on a moonlit beach. You should ask him."

She laughed out loud and made a face despite the fact that Roxie couldn't see her. "I will not ask the man to kiss me."

"You're just no fun. I bet he would. It's already romantic with him hurdling a fence to help you. Tell me he's single and that you're going to have a romance."

"Roxie, he's a diver. He owns a dive shop, for goodness gracious. According to the dive shop profile, he does all kinds of adventurous, risky hobbies. There is no way he would be attracted to a person like me. I have never taken a risk in my life. I get lightheaded at the sight of blood and it is just a miracle I don't pass out over it. I am *not* his type." She thought of the blonde who'd pushed him into the bay. Obviously beautiful, full of life, and probably passionate if pushing a man in the bay was any indication. Sammy Jo could see Jake with someone like that. Unless the woman was just a horrible person. Sammy Jo would never do any of that.

"Stop making assumptions."

"If by some chance he did ask me out, it wouldn't take long for him to realize we are not compatible. I'm boring on so many levels and he's not. No way could I hold a man like him."

It was true and she refused to kid herself into thinking otherwise. She was practical, if anything. He had seemed interested, but she knew she had nothing to offer a man like Jake Sinclair and it wouldn't take him long to figure that out.

"Hey, stop shortchanging yourself."

"I'm just being realistic." She watched him greet his morning group of divers. Four men and five females. While he was greeting them, he caught sight of her and raised his hand in greeting. Her heart fluttered. She lifted her hand and waved, and then looked away and forced herself not to read more into his smile than was there.

"He could be your man."

"He's not my man. He's the man who owns the dive shop next door. Who I might hire to give me dive lessons. So, can we talk about something else?"

"You always want to close off the conversation when it gets too close for comfort. And do not forget that you are there to come out of your cocoon and become a butterfly. You and Gram worked that list up together and you promised. Do you hear me?"

Sammy Jo's fingers tightened around the phone.

"Sammy Jo?"

She watched Jake talking with one of the women, saw the redhead toy with her long, red hair as she spoke to him. No, Sammy Jo could not compete with women like her. She had nothing to offer a man like Jake.

"Sams?"

"Yes, Roxie. I hear you."

"Good, because I made a promise to your gram too. And I'm going to keep mine to her, so be ready. My job is to help you get out there. My job is to hound you until you get out of your shell."

Sammy Jo dropped her forehead to her palm. "Why did I ever promise Gram that I would do the bucket list?"

"Because of one simple reason. You and I both know that in your heart, it is your deepest desire to have some adventure in your life. You just have to get some gumption, as Gram called it."

She sighed. "Right. But Roxie, now that I'm here,

I'm scared and gumption is scarce."

"And that's understandable. You've hidden inside walls until now, taking care of your grandparents and building a business online. Now you're stepping out and so that is totally understandable. But just like your gram used to say, you can get happy in the same pants you got scared in. Girlfriend, you can do this. *You can* and don't you forget it, okay? But while you're doing it, be kind to yourself. You deserve it."

She nodded and took a deep breath as she watched the boat with Jake and his group of merry adventurers' head out to sea.

One day, maybe she could be on that boat. *Maybe.*

The sun was setting on the bay with an amazing show of golden orange and vibrant pinks when Jake finished for the day. He'd had his new neighbor on his mind all day. He spotted Sammy Jo folding empty packing boxes outside her back door and he headed that way.

"How's the knee?" he called, walking down the sidewalk. She had obviously been unpacking all day because he'd spotted her at daybreak when he'd been heading out on his first dive.

Her smile was gentle and did funny things in his chest.

"It's fine," she said, her voice soft and enticing. "A little stiff, but I lived thanks to you."

"And I'm grateful I could help. I really felt bad about leaving you yesterday."

She looked startled. "Why, you were amazing. I told my friend, Roxie, how great you were when we were talking on the phone this morning. You helped me so much and I'm the one who is grateful you came along when you did. There is nothing to feel bad about."

"After I left you, I kept thinking about you having to move your things up to that apartment when you had a bum knee. I should have stayed."

"No, you shouldn't have. Contrary to how it seems, I can take care of myself. You are a busy guy, that's easy to see."

"Swamped, actually. But, luckily I made it through the day without getting dumped in the bay by any more disgruntled customers."

She laughed. "That's always a good thing. And I haven't tried to dive on the pavement anymore, so things are looking up for both of us. You had an early start this morning. Do you go out that early every morning?"

"Not every morning. But I enjoy it. I like morning jogs too, so I try to have two mornings a week that I start later. Do you jog?"

"That is actually something I do enjoy. I could do that without getting too far from home." She inhaled the salty air and stared out toward the ocean. As if it called to her, she walked, with a slightly stiff walk, toward the railing. He followed her, enjoying how her pale blue dress clung to her in the breeze. She looked as if she belonged with the bay; the colors and movement seemed to flow seamlessly with the surroundings. When she reached the railing, she placed both hands on it and studied the view.

He studied her. She was beautiful. "Why did you need to stay close to home? Or were you just afraid to get too far away?" She had a bucket list and she stayed near home. That was so far all he knew about her.

"I took care of my grandparents and I ran my online business, so I had a lot going on that kept me home," she said a little too quickly, as she turned from the water. "I better get back. I'm making some headway but I still have a good bit to go. My sign arrived and I want to see if I can get it up. Hanging it on the front of the store will make it feel official."

"I can hang that for you." He started toward her shop.

"No." She caught up to him, her expression full of alarm. "Really, I can't take your time again today."

He kept walking and noticed she limped as she was probably feeling some stiffness from that wounded knee. *All the more reason he should hang her sign.* "I don't mind. Besides, my mom would have a fit if she knew I didn't help my new neighbor hang her sign. She taught all her boys better than that."

"Okay, but I feel like I'm imposing." Her expression was tense.

"Only if you refused my offer." He winked at her hoping to ease the worry in her eyes.

Her lip twitched, then she chuckled softly. "You are persuasive."

"I try really hard." She was cute, and her soft chuckle curled deep in his chest like a purring kitten. "I want to do this." They stared at each other, a battle of wills. At last her lip twitched and he knew he'd won.

She cocked her head to the side. "Then could you please help me hang my sign."

He held open her door and shot her his best cocky grin. "I thought you would never ask."

Sammy Jo stared up at Jake on the ladder as he drilled a hole for the new bolts he'd insisted the sign needed. The sun was going down and the light from inside the shop was starting to cast a glow on the sidewalk. It was a nice evening. She tried to focus on that but it was not enough to distract her from the fact that her hunky neighbor was standing on the ladder helping her. It was difficult not to stare at him.

"There, the hooks are in." He climbed down the ladder and hopped off the last rung. "You ready to climb up there and hang that baby? I'll help hold it. You'd have had your hands full trying to hang this thing on your own with just that screwdriver you had to work with."

"You're right." She was trying very hard to ignore how standing close to Jake was affecting her. She hadn't minded watching him work but now he would be watching her. Feeling self-conscious and praying she didn't fall off the ladder, she took one end of the sign as he held the other and then she climbed up one rung at a time. The sign was only hanging from the low-slung awning which was only nine feet from the ground. She stopped climbing up the ladder and looked down at Jake. He held the ladder and her hips happened to be on level with his shoulders. She was all too aware of the man. Their gazes locked and her knees grew mushy, like her insides.

He was staring at her as if he were nervous. The idea was laughable. She did not make Jake Sinclair nervous. *No way. He made her nervous though.*

"Just hook each of those brackets on the sign to the hanger."

"Okay." She slipped the hook over the bolt and then, as he lifted his end of the sign, she leaned out from the ladder to slip the other hook over the second bolt. "There all done."

She climbed down the ladder, ready to be on solid ground again. He was holding the ladder and they were very close. Her heart rate was erratic as she paused on the bottom rung, at eye level with him.

"Congratulations. Your store is official. It's a good feeling isn't it. I remember how I felt when I hung my sign with my name on it. *Jakes Dive Shop*. It felt good."

She liked him. "It does feel great. I like having my name on my clothing. And business."

"Lovely You." His gaze searched hers. "It's a really nice name, Sammy-So-Lovely."

Butterflies erupted in her chest at his nickname for her. She could get used to hearing that. It gave her a thrill despite telling herself that he was just teasing her. But then, she looked at him and something in his eyes kept telling her he was feeling what she was feeling.

No way. That wasn't possible. She was really

kidding herself.

He liked adventure, to do things; the man not only enjoyed scuba diving, he enjoyed things like skydiving too. *He could not be interested in her.*

Seconds passed and she told herself to move away from him, but her body was not listening to her.

"Can I ask you something?" he asked at last, continuing to hold her mesmerized.

She nodded, trying to keep her gaze from dropping to his lips.

"Would you go swimming with me?"

Her brows dipped together. "Swimming?" She blinked hard. *Had he just asked her to swim with him?*

There was a chuckle in his words. "Yes, tomorrow after I get off. There's a small island just off the coast surrounded by clear, shallow water that's perfect for swimming. I thought if you were feeling adventurous, that I could take you out there and you could mark two things off of that bucket list that yours."

Her mouth went dry. "Mark things off." She swallowed hard.

"A boat ride and swimming in the ocean." He

smiled. "What do you say?"

"I, well, I've never been." She was stumbling over her words and repeating things they both already knew.

He chuckled. "But would you like to go? You need to swim in the ocean and make sure you don't get seasick before you make the next step of scuba diving."

Her stomach knotted. *He was offering to help her fulfill her major bucket list item, scuba diving. And he was so right: if she got seasick, how could she scuba dive?*

"Say yes. I can see it in your eyes that you want to." He smiled and melted all of her defenses.

"I feel like I've moved here and am intruding on your life. But if you're sure, then I'd love to go."

"Great. And you're not intruding."

"I just hope I don't throw up."

He laughed. "They make good meds for that these days. So, it's a yes?"

"Yes. I'll be ready." She couldn't stop the smile of excitement that burst to her lips from deep inside her. She felt almost giddy. Then he smiled and her chest tightened.

"Great. I'll see you then." He reached for the ladder. His arm brushed hers and sparked a tingle of awareness through her like wildfire.

She moved out of the way so he could get the ladder and then she watched him pick it up. His bicep flexed, reminding her of how strong he was. "Thank you for doing this, all of this."

He paused, holding the ladder, and there was a teasing light in his eyes. "No problem. It'll be fun."

Something about this man had her believing that it would be okay. She felt tremendous trepidation but excitement filled her too. "I'll be ready."

His smiled deepened. "Then it's a date. I'll see you tomorrow."

A date… Ha, if only she could be so lucky. She was not kidding herself, and totally understood he was simply helping her out. The man probably felt sorry for her after reading her bucket list.

No, she wasn't kidding herself, and absolutely knew this was not a real date. He was just being helpful. That's who he was; a very helpful guy.

CHAPTER FOUR

The next afternoon, Jake got the last dive group back to the dock in record time. Once again, he'd had Sammy Jo on his mind all day and he was ready to take her out on the water. He saw her coming down the dock as the last of his group left and his pulse skipped erratically. She wore a cover-up that came to her knees. The soft yellow outfit was modest and had him thinking about how pretty she was again. She looked like a ray of sunshine as she walked toward him with a beautiful smile.

He wasn't sure how it had happened, but he really

looked forward to seeing her pretty face each day. And taking her out on her first boat ride made him happy because she looked so happy.

"Hey pretty lady, you ready to come ride with me?" She beamed and his pulse careened recklessly.

"Honestly, I have been like a kid all day. I am so excited. But a little freaked out too."

He hopped from the boat to the pier and it took everything in him not to hug her. "Totally understandable. But relax. We're going to take the twenty-three-foot ride today instead of the *Hopper.*" He crossed the pier and jumped into the smaller boat. He held out a hand to Sammy Jo.

She stared at the boat. "You call this a small boat?"

He grinned. "Yeah, compared to others, but it is very sea-worthy."

She took his hand, tingles shooting up his arm at her touch. She stepped onto the edge of the boat; it rocked and she slipped as she moved to step down into the boat.

"I've got you." He grabbed her around the waist

and set her on her feet. She smelled nice, sweet and tempting. "You'll get your sea legs in a second."

"I hope so. It's rocking. I'll have to adjust to that feeling."

"Yes, you will." He took his hands away, though it was tough to do so. "If you'll go sit on that bench by the steering wheel, I'll untie us and then we'll head out."

She did as he asked, moving slowly to the bench. He moved to turn the key and fired up the twin motors and then headed to the front of the boat. "This boat will get us close to the island I'm taking you to. It moves in shallow water easily." He untied the front then went and untied the back; then he moved to stand beside her. "You can stand beside me and lean your hips against the bench seat or you can sit on it. Either way is fine."

She leaned against the seat and held onto the handle on the side of the dashboard. "I'll try it this way at first."

"Sounds good. Here we go." He pointed the boat out toward the mouth of the bay and then pushed the throttle forward and got them moving.

He slid a glance at Sammy Jo and saw she was smiling into the wind. Her eyes glittered with happiness as she looked at him. "What do you think?" he asked over the wind.

"I love this!"

"So, do I. Lean back and hang on. Let's do this."

The wind whipped into Sammy Jo's eyes and tugged some strands of her hair from the clasp she'd pulled it back with. It was a losing battle as the strands played around her face, whipped about by the breeze rushing around her. She was filled with exhilaration and a sense of pure joy as the boat cut through the waves, passing sailboats and yachts. She could get used to this. Jake slowed the boat to watch a pontoon plane take off. It bounded over the water and then lifted into the air.

"That looks fun too." She leaned close so Jake could hear her.

He smiled at her. "It is."

When the boat didn't veer from its path toward them—her heart thundered as she watched it race over the water toward them. "Is it going to hit us?" She grabbed Jake's arm just as the small plane lifted from the water and sailed easily over their head into the blue sky.

She swung around, snapping her hands over her eyes as the plane dipped its left wing toward them before it rode in a long arch then flew back over them and then down the coast. She whirled to look at Jake. "I thought it was going to hit us."

His smile widened. "He wasn't on the right trajectory to hit us, though it would look that way. That's a friend of mine who enjoys giving me a hard time and buzzing my customers. I get him back sometimes." He grinned. "It really just seems like he's gonna hit you when he's actually not on target for you."

"Well, that's a relief. You could tell a girl, you know."

"And spoil the excitement of the moment for you?"

"Or the thrill you get from watching me nearly hyperventilate." She laughed. "And here I was just thinking you are a really nice guy."

"I am a nice guy. I'm helping you check things off your bucket list. My buddy can take you up in that plane, if you want to add that to your list."

She stared at him in dismay. "Are you serious?"

"I am."

"I'll think about it. My bucket list is a work in progress."

"Yeah, but it's cool you have one. I want to see this bucket list fulfilled. You're the first person I've ever known who actually wrote one down. I like that. It's an adventure in itself."

They stared at each other.

"Turtle!" he exclaimed, swerving the boat and sending Sammy Jo flying up against him. He wrapped an arm around her to steady her. "Sorry about that. I didn't want to hit the poor turtle. It would have injured him or killed him. Are you okay?" He stared down at her and her heart was racing against his.

She nodded, feeling his heart beating just as hard

through his thin T-shirt. "I'm fine. Thanks for saving the turtle," she said breathlessly and then pushed away from him to cling to the handle to steady herself, and to keep from accidentally, on purpose, falling against him again.

She thought about her bucket list. Her thoughts snagged on one item.

"Hang on over there. It's time to get you in the water. One island coming up." He smiled at her.

Her pulse raced and for a moment she let herself dream. The man was funny and amazing and she now had added him to her list... Instead of it reading *kissing a man on a moonlit beach*, it was now *kiss Jake Sinclair on a moonlit beach*.

A girl could dream.

Jake wasn't sure why Sammy Jo affected him like no one else ever had, but he did know that she had something that pulled him in. Maybe it was her quiet spirit. Just looking at her gave him a sense of calm that he wasn't used to. He was an on-the-go, fast-pace loving guy and so it was startling to look in her deep green eyes and just want to stay in a holding pattern. She'd probably think he was weird if he just stared at her hours on end, though.

It was something he'd never experienced before. He was totally willing and ready to figure out how this dynamic was going to work.

For now, he was enjoying the expression of joy on her face as he drove the boat over the blue waters of the coast he loved. *Why had she never taken a risk? Why had she never opened a store?* These were questions about her that filled his thoughts.

"Are you having fun?" he asked after they had ridden in silence for a few minutes.

Her eyes lit up like Fourth of July fireworks exploding. "I *love* it. I really do."

Her excitement drew him like a moth. Over her shoulder, he saw movement in the water. He touched her arm and leaned toward her. "There." He pointed past her toward the pair of porpoises swimming not far from the boat, keeping pace as they glided through the water.

Her gaze caught his. She hesitated and then turned to see what he was pointing at. "Oh wow," she gasped. "They are fantastic."

His heart had picked up, being so close to her. Her hair tickled his nose and she had pressed back, probably without even realizing she was doing it, but her back was pressed against his shoulder as she watched the porpoises jumping from the water. He had the urge to wrap an arm around her shoulders and pull her closer. But breathing in the scent of her, he reluctantly kept his hand on the steering wheel and drove, slowing down to stay near the dolphins. She pushed her strands of escaped hair out of her face and held it back with one hand as she studied the sleek gray mammals.

"I could watch them all day. They are so cute."

He could watch *her* all day. "Good, because you're going to get to swim with them. Or at least near them. Do you see that tiny patch of green in the distance? That's the island we're heading to and the porpoises hang out around the island."

She spun to look directly at him. "Really? They'll

actually come near us?"

"Sometimes."

Her eyes flared. "Thank you so much for bringing me here."

He felt suddenly about ten feet tall. "Anything for the lady," he said, wanting more than anything in that moment to kiss her. He also realized in that moment that he was in way over his head where his new neighbor was concerned. He had never had this strong of an attraction to someone before.

It was a place he had never really thought he would be in. It took his breath away.

"Is everything okay?" Her smile faded to a slightly baffled expression.

He gave himself a mental shake. "Yeah, sure. Everything is perfect."

"Okay. For a minute there, you looked worried."

"Worried, me? Nah." He gave a reassuring grin and hoped it looked genuine.

At last she seemed to accept his words and turned away to stare at the island, he breathed a sigh of relief. He raked a hand through his short hair and fought to regain his footing before he fell straight off the cliff he was suddenly teetering on.

And he was most certainly teetering. Falling without a parachute seemed more accurate.

Overwhelmed by the beauty of her surroundings, *and* the amazing man who had taken time out of his day to bring her here, Sammy Jo watched the porpoises play in the water surrounding the tiny picture-perfect island. Never in a million years would she have dreamed this day up.

And he'd come up with it on a whim.

He slowed the boat and they eased into shallow waters near the tiny island.

"It's so clear and such a gentle turquoise." Enthralled, she leaned over the edge and looked down. The variations of water colors fascinated her. Different depths gave different shades. It was amazing. She could clearly see the rocks on the bottom. She felt like she was in a dream where everything was breathtaking and so different from her life four months ago. "How deep is it right now?"

"It's about ten feet here. We'll move in to about four feet and I'll anchor up."

"It is wild to find this little island in the middle of nowhere and with its own little expanse of white sandy beach."

He had put his shades on and she could no longer see his eyes. "There are small places like this dotted all over the coast. This one is special to me because of the porpoises that hang out around it. It also is where we used to come for family picnics growing up."

She stared at him with wonder filled eyes. "Family picnics on an island. I can't imagine that…" her voice trailed off and she looked back to the island. "I still can't believe I'm here now. I'm thrilled just seeing them."

He had been moving the boat slowly toward the shore and now he shut off the engine and walked to the front of the boat and unhooked the anchor. It dropped into the water and he fed the chain overboard until it caught. He hadn't missed the longing in her voice when she'd spoken of the family picnic. He had taken those times for granted since his family loved everything about Windswept Bay. And everything about being a big family.

Once he let go of the anchor, he turned toward her and grinned. "Okay, all set. Your own personal swimming pool. Complete with porpoises." He pointed behind her and she turned just in time to see the sleek gray dolphins jump from the water, as if copying each other.

She brought her hands up to her cheeks and watched in awe. "Look at their silky gray bodies gleaming in the sunlight."

Jake came to stand beside her at the edge of the boat. He loved her excitement. "They're acrobats of the sea."

"I just can't believe you brought me here." She placed her hand on his arm and blinked as tears pooled in her eyes. "I didn't even have this on my list and suddenly here I am, about to get into the gorgeous water and swim with these beautiful creatures." She blinked hard but tears ran down her cheeks. "I'm sorry about the tears. It's crazy, I don't even know why I'm tearing up. Except that I was just so surprised and so excited."

"Don't cry." He stepped toward her, concerned gaze locked on the tear that slipped down her cheek and he startled her by cupping her jaw and gently brushing it away with the pad of his thumb. Every cell in his body called for him to hold onto her. To make everything right for her, because something about Sammy Jo's life seemed very off to him.

"I didn't mean to make you cry but if it's good tears then that's okay. Are they good tears?"

Sammy Jo tried not to lean her face into his hand. It felt so good there against her skin. "It's good tears" she whispered, longing to feel his arms around her as they'd been that day he'd come to her rescue.

His grin grew and his eyes twinkled. "Thank goodness for four sisters who taught me that sometimes girls cry good tears. If not for that, then I'd have been worried."

"You did very good." Emotion caused her voice to wobble.

"Good, when I say I'm going to help you do something, I want to do it right. But this shows me that you definitely need to get out more. Are you ready to get in the water?" He dropped his hand and smiled with what could only be described as a mischievous grin.

The man made it hard to think straight. "I'm ready. I feel like a child on Christmas morning. I'm more than ready."

"Then let's do this." He stripped off his T-shirt and she forgot to breathe for a moment as the sun kissed his tanned, muscled torso. He tossed the shirt on the dash of the boat and then placed his hands on his hips. "Okay, your turn. You aren't going to swim in that cover-up, are you?"

"Oh, right." Trying not to be self-conscious, she pulled the cover-up over her head and laid it on the dash beside his shirt. She was glad she'd chosen her yellow one-piece, because she knew there was no way her body could ever compete with his. Or the scuba diving, string bikini-clad girl who'd pushed him into the bay that first day.

She forced herself to meet his twinkling eyes. "I'm ready."

"Yes, you are." His eyes held hers. "You can swim, right?"

"I can swim, though it's been awhile. And never in the ocean." Of course, he knew that, she was rambling.

"I'm glad you can swim. I'll teach you to snorkel today and that will help get you ready to take dive lessons."

"Snorkeling sounds fun…but maybe scuba diving could come later."

"We'd use a pool to get that process started before taking you out to a real dive. But we could have you ready in a few weeks."

"Oh, that would be quick."

"Yeah, it doesn't take as long as you think to get you ready to dive with an instructor."

She fought down the panic that threatened to set

in. "Really, there's no rush. But the snorkeling is something I am adding to the bucket list. And, you know, I hadn't meant for you to have to take on my whole list."

"Hey, it's fun. I'm enjoying helping you," he said and then he dove into the water in a perfectly executed shallow dive over the edge of the boat.

She gasped and lunged to the side of the boat. Thankfully he'd dove onto the far side of the boat where the water was still some deeper.

He came up almost instantly, water swinging off of him as he shook his head and grinned up at her. "Come on in. The water is perfect. If you don't want to jump in, then come back here to the back of the boat and step on the platform."

She couldn't move for a moment as he swam to the back and waited for her. It was as if he knew where she would head. And absolutely, there was no way she was attempting to dive in after his perfect showcase. Feeling shaky and keyed up, she stepped cautiously over the edge to the small platform next to the motor. He grinned up at her and held his hand up to her and she really, really thought about pinching herself to make sure she wasn't dreaming this entire trip. Maybe she was Alice in Wonderland and she'd fallen down a rabbit hole.

She wanted to do this. Nerves tumbled through her as she slipped her hand into his, inhaled deeply, then jumped, feet first, into the water with him. Not graceful but it would have to do.

She plunged beneath the water and then felt the tug of his fingers as her toes touched sand and she kicked up to burst from the water smiling. She hadn't swum in so long but thankfully it all came back to her as she moved her legs to keep her head above water. Not that she needed to worry or anything; the man was all smiles as he tugged her fingers and swam toward the shore, towing her with him.

A moment later, he stopped swimming and stood. "We can touch here. Relax."

Her feet sank into the sand just as a porpoise whizzed by like a torpedo. She screamed because she hadn't been expecting it and moved toward Jake.

He laughed and pulled her close, wrapping his

arms protectively around her. "It's okay. It's just a friendly porpoise."

She laughed shakily. "I thought it was a shark," she gasped. Her heart thundered as she looked up at him.

He grinned. "Nope, just your friendly porpoise."

"Right. I just wasn't expecting it and it startled me."

His grin deepened. "I am not complaining. You can jump into my arms any time."

Only then did she realize that she was plastered against the man like a second skin. His heart was pounding against hers and his lips were so close. "Oh..." Her voice trailed off as she had the sudden overwhelming desire to kiss him. *What was he going to think if she kept throwing herself at him?*

"Not a problem, at all," he murmured. His gaze dropped to her lips. His brows bent slightly and then he set her on her feet. "Are you ready to walk on your very own personal piece of paradise for the afternoon?"

Had he thought about kissing her like she had

thought about kissing him?

"Yes," she blurted, needing space, baffled by what had just happened. She took off toward the white sandy beach. She needed land beneath her feet, and she needed it now.

Because right now she felt as if she were stuck in the deep end of the pool and was floundering to keep a grasp of reality.

CHAPTER FIVE

"I still can't believe you haven't ever come to the beach." Jake watched as Sammy Jo pulled the facemask from her face with the snorkel dangling from the connector. She had taken to snorkeling almost instantly. Here he'd thought she was going to be timid and maybe even afraid. But no, she'd listened intently to his instructions and then she'd put on her mask, wrapped her mouth around the snorkel mouthpiece and dipped her face into the water, following his directions to perfection. Once she'd done that, she looked up at him, water dripping from her wet hair, and she'd laughed with joy. The woman laughed more than anyone he'd ever known.

"I love this. This is going to be great," she said after pulling the mouthpiece from her mouth. "And the fact that the porpoise came up to us *two* times was fascinating to me. Hands down amazing."

"They know a pretty lady when she's near." That got him a blush. "We're going to have to head back soon."

"Okay." She walked out of the water and sank down on the sand. He followed her. "I just can't get over how vibrantly colored everything is. The yellow fish pop like neon lemons and the orange and purples—it was just amazing."

"Wait until you scuba dive. You'll be even closer to them. It's a whole other world down there."

She looked nervous suddenly. "Yes, well, no hurry there. I loved today. Thank you so much."

"You're welcome." He grinned, excited about the thought of taking her diving. "I thought today would be a good day to get the preliminaries out of the way."

Preliminaries. He'd gotten more out of the way

than he'd realized. He had had to fight off the desire to kiss the mermaid smiling at him. He wanted to know more about her. For starters, if she adapted so quickly to this adventure, why had she never done it before? Yeah, she'd said she'd taken care of her grandparents and then she had her work. He'd felt then that there was more to it than she had wanted to say and he felt even more sure of it now.

"Why haven't you done something like this before?"

"My home in Texas was four hours from the nearest beach. Which meant if I went I'd be gone all day, if I were to make it back to the house before nightfall. And I couldn't be gone all day."

He didn't understand why she was so tied down. "But why were you so tied down?"

She glanced longingly at her snorkel then back at him. "Because my grandmother needed me to help with Granddad. Then later, she needed me to take care of both of them. My granddad was a war hero, and he came home an invalid. He'd lost both his legs in the war and he also suffered from terrible bouts of vertigo and PTSD. They needed me."

"Wow, I'm sorry." Jake felt for the older man. "That's a rough break." He didn't talk much about his time as a SEAL but he'd been one of the lucky ones. He'd had plenty of close calls, and so had his brothers Max and Trent. But they'd all made it out. He counted his blessings every day.

"My granddad served his country proudly and didn't talk about it much. But he didn't do well with others around. He and Gram raised me most of my life. I don't know what would have happened to me if they hadn't taken me in."

"Why did they have to do that? Other than, of course, that they loved you."

"I never knew my dad. Not even a name on my birth certificate. I don't normally talk about that." She frowned. "It's personal."

"It's not your fault the man wasn't around." He wanted to make her feel comfortable. And he felt good that she'd confided in him.

Her eyes held his and he watched them soften. "Right. He might not even have known he'd created a baby. Anyway, my mom was an addict and…they and the courts took me from her to save me. She died of an overdose not long after that."

He hadn't expected that. Their gazes locked. "That's rough. I'm glad you had them. This world would be far worse right now if not for all the good grandparents out there stepping up to help with their grandchildren."

"I know. I was blessed to have them. And I am so grateful I was able to help them when they needed me. They meant the world to me. Gram taught me how to sew at an early age and that's given me this joy of my own business."

"That's cool. How did that get started?" He was curious about her and wanted to know as much as she would share.

"I started making my own clothes by the time I was in high school. People started asking me where I was getting my outfits and so I started making clothes for friends too. I came home and then made a website and Gram came up with the name. We were making plans, dreaming dreams, and really enjoying ourselves.

And then she had the stroke. It was a bad stroke and it left her pretty paralyzed. I was very lucky that she lived at all." Her voice wobbled with emotion.

Jake placed a hand on hers. "I'm so sorry."

She shot him a bittersweet smile. "So anyway, as you see, there wasn't time for me to have adventures, because after that I had both of them to take care of. Though I did have some help come in a few days a week to help with Gram's rehab."

"That was good." He couldn't imagine having no free time. But he could tell she thought it was no big deal. She had a wonderful heart, it was easy to see.

"When Gram realized she probably wasn't going to get better, she came up with the bucket list. She hated for me to be so tied down and wanted me to look forward to what I would do one day. I wasn't keen on it at first. But she loved to play the bucket list game and she got to where she could talk and I could understand her. When she had another stroke after Granddad passed away, she made me promise that I would move to Windswept Bay. This is where she met my granddad. So, it was agreed I would move here. And that I would start fulfilling our bucket list."

"*Our* bucket list?"

She smiled. "Yes, my list is very personal, as you can imagine. And I may not ever fulfill everything on it, but each thing I check off will be for Gram." Her words were thick with emotion.

She was still grieving, he realized. "That's a wonderful story, in a tragic way. Your grandmother cared for you deeply and it sounds like your granddad did too. I'm so very sorry for your losses."

"Thank you. They were there for me when I needed them. So, it went both ways. I loved them deeply."

"How long ago did you lose them?"

"My granddad passed away almost a year ago and I lost Gram four months ago."

"Not long at all."

"No, but I didn't hesitate to implement our plan. I was afraid if I didn't, I might back out. My friend Roxie helped push me to do it too. It was a promise she'd made to my gram. So here I am. Determined to open my horizons."

"I want to help you with as many things as you need me to help you achieve or want me to help you achieve. If you'll let me." He might not have all the spare time in the world but he would find it. He wanted to help Sammy Jo more than anything he'd ever wanted in his life. If anyone deserved help, it was her.

"Okay, I would like that. If you have time."

"I have time. Now, we better get in the boat and head home. We'll get started on dive lessons next week."

"Oh, really, no real rush on that one."

He pulled her to her feet and into his arms. He gave her a quick hug and a gentle kiss to the top of her head. "It's going to be fun. We're going to make your gram proud."

She chuckled. "She would have loved you."

"That sounds like very high praise. Thanks."

"It is. She would also wish you luck."

He chuckled. "Won't need it. You're going to love

it." As they headed back to the boat, he got the feeling something significant had just shifted in his world and it revolved around Sammy Jo.

Sammy Jo got her shop opened by the end of the week. She was pleased with the look of the place, with the accessories and her designs; she felt excitement that shoppers would love them too. She had Jake on her mind every day since he'd taken her out in his boat. She barely knew him, and yet she felt as if she had always known him. *How was that?*

Her gram had said the first time she'd seen her granddad on the beach at the Windswept Bay Resort, that something about him had called to her. Not one to believe in love at first sight, she wouldn't let herself believe in it at first. But her gram soon changed her belief when she couldn't stop herself from spending every moment with Grandad and she didn't want to. From that moment of realization, until the day he died he was the love of her life.

Sammy Jo couldn't get that off of her mind as she

sat on her little balcony at night and worked on projects and enjoyed her new life…but she also ached for her grandparents. But her thoughts always went back to Jake. And it had done so from the moment she'd first met him. Or first saw him, leaping over the railing and rushing to her rescue. But did *she* believe in love at first sight? She wasn't ready to do that. She knew she liked him. So, she totally believed in *like* at first sight. She didn't really know him…or did she— the voice in her head protested. She knew he was kind, compassionate, a strong hero. He made her laugh and he'd gone out of his way to help her in every way he could.

What was there not to like? Something about him spoke to something inside her and that couldn't be denied. Right now, she ached to see him getting off his boat, waving at her and smiling broadly up at her.

On Tuesday evening, Jake took her to a pool as they'd decided to do after the snorkeling adventure. She was really nervous about it but wouldn't admit it to him. He really wanted to help her. He taught her how to wear the mask and the oxygen tanks and, despite the fact that her chest felt as if it were going to explode, when she actually crouched down in the pool beneath the water's surface, she managed to hold her panic in and not completely freak out.

She would do this. She would. It just might not be as easy as Jake made out that it would be.

When he drove her back to her apartment after their lesson, he walked her to her door.

"I was wondering if you'd like to go out?" he asked. "For dinner, on a date?"

A date. She had been enjoying his company but this totally took her by surprise. Probably because no matter how she sometimes thought he looked at her, she just couldn't believe that he was actually interested in her in that way. They were so different. She was, after all, kind of living a lie. She was playing at becoming adventurous. She wasn't really and surely he understood that.

She was an impostor, pure and simple, and she needed to remember that in order to keep her head from living in the clouds. This amazingly capable, handsome, unbelievable guy could not really be interested in dating her. "A date? Me?"

"Of course, you." He looked baffled now. "Who else would I be asking?"

Her cheeks warmed. "I don't know. You just caught me off guard. Sure, that would be fun." Her pulse raced and panic threatened. Once he realized she was not adventurous enough to keep up with him, he would move on and then what would become of their friendship? It was a risk on so many levels that started with the risk of being hurt when he realized that she was just an ordinary female who truly had nothing in common with him. The man could have any woman he wanted. Women probably melted at his feet. *What did he see in her?*

It was one thing to dream about a man like Jake but another to actually believe it could happen. It was dangerous and risky.

"Can you go tonight? I know it's last minute, but I just found out a great band is playing at Paradise Grill later tonight. I thought it would be fun and a way to welcome you to the community now that you're settled in after a week of a lot of hard work on your part. My friend, Bert, owns the place. It's on the beach, has great food and entertainment. And it's going to be a gorgeous full moon tonight."

Her heart skipped. "Could we walk on the beach?" She smiled, because she had been looking forward to fulfilling that particular bucket list item. She knew it would be a stretch to get the kiss but a girl could hope.

"You're reading my mind. I thought we could mark another item off your bucket list."

"I can be dressed in an hour. Is that good?" She was going for this. If by some miracle he snuck in a quick kiss, she could probably die and go to heaven. This was craziness. But she suddenly felt very reckless. And that was just so not her. *Could it be that he was actually rubbing off on her?*

"Perfect. I'll go clean up and be back." And with that, he turned and walked away.

And Sammy Jo melted right into the chair by the door.

Her insides muddled together in knots. *She was*

going walking on a beach with Jake on a moonlit night. And if God were smiling down on her, maybe she could mark off being kissed by a man on a moonlit beach.

Specifically, kissed by Jake. *Because suddenly she knew no other man would do.*

CHAPTER SIX

Paradise Grill was busy as Jake held open the door and let Sammy Jo enter. She looked beautiful tonight in one of her soft pink creations. He gave the hostess his name, having made a reservation for the outside deck. As they were following the hostess to their seat, he paused at the bar area where Bert was visiting with customers.

When Bert saw him, he excused himself and came over. "Jake, what's up, man?"

"Just came out for some good food and entertainment. This is Sammy Jo. She's new in town."

"Nice to meet you. But are you sure about hanging out with this fella?" Bert grinned. "Maybe you need to look into this a little bit better. A lot of good guys in this town, but I'm not sure about the one that you're with."

"Thanks a lot. With friends like you, I don't need enemies." Jake grinned.

"I think I'm doing okay." Sammy Jo laughed. "But thanks for the advice. I'll keep an eye on him."

"Aw, I'm just giving him a hard time. Jake's a good guy."

"Finally. Thanks for the endorsement." Jake then placed a hand on Sammy Jo's back and nudged her to follow the hostess. "Talk to you in a bit," he said to Bert, who grinned and gave him a thumbs-up.

They were just sitting down at their table when his sister Cali and her husband Grant came up. His sister had a gleam in her eye that told him she was very happy to see him.

"Hi, I'm Cali Ellington, Jake's older sister, and this is my husband, Grant. You must be Sammy Jo." She held her hand out to Sammy Jo.

"I am, but how did you guess?"

Cali smiled from Sammy Jo to Jake. "He told me about your boutique. And he even said your clothing was really pretty. Do you know how much that got my attention? For Jake Sinclair, macho man himself, to say clothing is pretty was a very strong endorsement."

Sammy Jo blushed the color of her pale-pink dress. "Thank you." She looked at Jake.

"I'm just stating facts. She's wearing one of her dresses right now," he said looking at Cali.

"And it is beautiful." Cali's gaze swept over the dress. "Would you ever care to put some things at the gift shop at Windswept Bay Resort? We're always looking for specialty items and would love to give you some exposure."

Sammy Jo's expression was of shock. "You would do that? That would be amazing. I read about the resort before I moved here. My grandmother had described it to me in detail because she actually met my granddad at that resort. And they came back later and were engaged there. It's been a long time, but I planned on coming and visiting to see where their love story began. I just haven't had a chance yet."

"That is a wonderful story," Cali said. "Our grandparents started the resort and then our parents took over. It's just in the last year and a half my sisters and I took it over. We've done renovations but essentially kept the essence of how it looked from the beginning. So hopefully it will resemble what your grandmother described to you. So, let's have lunch and talk, and not just business but as friends. We'd love to welcome you to the area. It's a wonderful place and we're glad to have you as a new neighbor."

Sammy Jo was touched. "I'd love that." This was the reason she wanted a physical store: for the companionship she might find in a community. She'd been isolated enough and an online business was, at least for her, a solitary endeavor.

"Shame on you, Jake. You should have taken her to the resort for dinner."

He laughed. "You know as well as I do that if I'd come to the resort, it would be all over town that I'd taken Sammy Jo out."

Grant gave a dry laugh. "You think your sisters weren't going to hear about it anyway?"

"A guy can only hope."

"And so can your sisters. I'll call you tomorrow, Sammy Jo. Or better yet, if I can, I'll drop by. You two enjoy your evening."

After they walked away, Jake leaned back in his chair with a sigh. "I guess you figured out I have some nosy sisters. And yes, I try to have a little privacy but it is not easy with four sisters. Cali is the oldest and then I have Jillian, Shar, and Olivia. They're triplets."

"Wow, triplets. I think it would be wonderful to have siblings."

"Don't forget that I also have four brothers. I could easily share a few with you."

He was funny. "Your parents might mind if you did that."

"If Mom and Dad thought they could find out anything serious about my love life, they'd be all for it. At this point, I'm the last holdout."

"I hardly qualify as your love life. This is our first

date and it does fit in with helping me achieve my bucket list. I'm guessing that means they're pressuring you?"

He stared at her for a long moment, contemplating whether to touch her love life comment or let it ride for now. "They wouldn't say so, but I'm feeling the pressure. But I'll do that when I'm ready. No rush. This is our first actual date, and I'm not disappointed in it so far. Are you?" He'd said more than he'd planned but giving the same answer he always gave just didn't feel right. He was feeling something new and different with Sammy Jo. Just the slightest touch of her hand sent his adrenaline into warp speed and he felt as if he were skiing down a mountainside on one ski without poles. And they'd yet to make it to the romantic walk on the beach. Anticipation held him captive and had him forcing himself to take his time eating and listening to the music in the background.

But he was ready to be done with this meal and

head out there now.

Dinner had been so nice but there was a tension between them that had Sammy Jo's insides knotted up. As they walked from the deck out onto the beach, she paused to just take in the way the moon shimmered on the water. She'd walked on the beach in the daytime already and loved to feel the sand beneath her bare feet. She slipped her sandals off and let them dangle from her fingertips while her toes sank into the gritty sand.

"I just can't get over how beautiful it is," she said as they walked to the water's edge.

She struggled with the knowledge that he'd read her bucket list and knew that, embarrassingly, being kissed on a moonlit beach by a man was part of the list. Her nerves were shaky and now, she shot him a hesitant smile. "Now that I've felt sand beneath my feet, I can't get enough of it."

"The beach fits you," he said, over the sound of the surf. He caught a strand of her hair being buffeted by the wind and tucked it behind her ear. "You look happy."

She couldn't move. "I am. I mean, I miss my grandparents something fierce, but I'm happy." She had a vision of kissing him and heat swept through her. She was thankful for some protection in the low light, because she was pretty certain she'd just turned scarlet.

He reached for her hand. "I'm glad you like the sand and the beach. It likes you. You're a beautiful woman, Sammy Jo, and in the moonlight, you're breathtaking. So, let's walk." He shot her what could only be described as a wicked smile. "That *is* on the bucket list."

She would have laughed but she was stuck on the fact that he just said she was beautiful. Heat from his touch sent tingles along her arm and his words had her mind stumbling. She could fall so hard for this man. *Don't get carried away, Sammy Jo. You'll get your heart broken.*

They walked in companionable silence, listening to the ebb and flow of the tide and following the glow of the moon. They passed other couples enjoying the evening, some walking and some enjoying a kiss.

She was glad the crashing waves were loud because they helped cover up the drumbeat of her heart.

"You said your grandparents met on the beach at the resort."

"Yes. My gram was there for a work-related weekend. My granddad was visiting friends. They met looking for seashells. Somehow, they shared their first kiss on the beach later and fell in love.

"When they left here, they continued the romance then came back and got engaged then married soon after. They always held a special place in their hearts for Windswept Bay, even though later it just wasn't possible for them to return."

"So, do you think that you're here in Windswept Bay to relive your grandmother's dreams for her or is there part of you that would be here if it were strictly for you?"

She thought about that. His hand tightened on hers. "I think it's a little of both. I'm trying to start my own history. Yes, much of my bucket list was created by me and Gram as a fun project and there really isn't much on it that is really risky. However, by making that bucket list, I think I was also looking for the fresh start it might give me if I could find the courage to achieve just some of the items on it. Beginning here on these beautiful beaches where my grandparents' love story began seemed fitting. It makes me happy. So, I have no regrets about coming here."

"I'm glad. You fit here. You'll like my sisters and they'll help you get to know the business community. They know everybody."

"I'm excited. So, tell me about your family. Everyone is married?"

"Yep. It started with my brother-in-law, Grant Ellington. He came to paint some sea life murals at the resort and, much like the story of your grandparents, he and Cali fell in love. And it seemed after that, my siblings started falling like dominos. It's been a really busy time. But…" He paused and turned toward her, gently tugging her toward him. "Right now, I'm kind of understanding everything a little more than I had. I think you are lovely, Sammy Jo. And I'm glad you're here." His eyes sparkled in the moonlight and her knees melted. "There is a kiss on your bucket list, right?"

His words sent a tingle up her spine. She froze, despite having barely thought of anything but that kiss on the list. She now was so embarrassed. "Yes, but it doesn't matter."

He frowned. "It doesn't? Are you sure about that?" He bent his head toward her.

Her breath caught. "N-no. It feels…it feels like begging."

He cocked his head to the side and his gaze got a predatory glint in it. "You're not begging. And believe me, I'm not feeling charitable at the moment."

She was having a hard time keeping her breathing steady. Her pulse pounded in her temple. "You don't have to—"

He cupped her face. "Yes, I do. I've had this moment on my mind ever since I first saw you. Believe me, I do have to be the one to fulfill that item on your bucket list." And then he dipped his head to hers.

The world started spinning, and she reached for him to steady herself. One of his hands dropped as he wrapped his arm around her and held her steady. He pulled her close while his other hand tangled in her hair. Her shoes dropped to the sand as her fingers dug into his sides and her knees went weak.

Emotions crashed like waves as her lips parted for his lips and she found herself being swept away by the feel of his kiss. Every fiber of her body burned as she melted against him. This was better than anything she could have imagined. More than she'd known to expect. She wanted…she wanted *what*?

Her brain couldn't form coherent thoughts. And then suddenly, Jake tensed then pulled away. He looked as dazed as she felt. The moon played across the hard planes of his face, casting shadows in his eyes.

She was sure she was imagining the dazed part. She might be new to this kissing game but he certainly wasn't. After a moment, he blinked. "Well, we wiped that one off your list."

The list. Right. "Yes," she said, still breathless and trying to regain some sense of composure. "I think we did, or you did. You could go into the bucket list business with that kind of kiss." *Lame but it was all she could think of.* She couldn't say what she was really thinking, which was *wow, just wow.*

His brows met and his expression grew serious. "That was some kiss. Maybe we better go back."

He picked up her sandals and handed them to her then took her other hand and they started back. *It had been some kiss but that was all he had to say?* She was confused. They walked back in silence, the spell broken. *Was he having second thoughts about having kissed her?*

She told herself not to overreact. It wasn't as if he had told her he was going to walk around the beach kissing her and fall in love with her. No, he had just said he was going to help her fulfill her bucket list, or at least part of it, and it was a moonlit walk and the kiss had been part of that.

The falling in love part was on her list but not something to snap her fingers and make happen. That was unrealistic, so what was her problem?

He wasn't the falling in love kind of guy. He wasn't the marrying kind. At least not right now. And she had better remember that or she knew she'd get hurt.

CHAPTER SEVEN

Jake went jogging the next morning. After he and Sammy Jo said goodnight. After the kiss that knocked him off his feet.

After dropping her off at her door, he'd hightailed it back down her stairs like a puppy with his tail between his legs. *What had he been thinking?* Since the first day he'd spotted her standing in the doorway of her shop, it had been as if he'd been functioning in a dream. Driven by something he'd never been driven by. And he'd wanted to be the man who kissed her on the beach.

And then he'd kissed her. And his world had tilted and suddenly, he was scrambling backward like a man on a slippery slide to another dimension. Was he ready for the emotions that had slammed into him as he'd kissed Sammy Jo?

The question reverberated through him with every thud of his running shoes slapping against the pavement along the ocean drive where he would meet up with his brother Trent for their weekly Saturday morning jog.

He couldn't clear his head. A kiss was a kiss; always had been. Until last night. He had wanted to kiss Sammy Jo in the moonlight for her bucket list. He just hadn't thought about the impact. He hadn't been able to bear the thought of Sammy Jo kissing someone else. He'd wanted that bucket list item all for himself.

He had never felt what he felt when his lips touched hers. It was as if something inside him had come alive, as if she intertwined throughout him and filled him. She had shaken him to his core and he didn't know what to do, or how to react to what he was feeling. So, instead, he'd shut down.

He tried to block it. Tried to pretend nothing had been different or special. Tried to be casual. But he knew that she knew something was wrong. She'd been very quiet on the ride home. He had been very quiet too, though he had started to say a few things but shut down in the end.

He'd told her goodnight and as lame as it was, he'd kissed her on her forehead before he'd left her. He just touched her cheek, backed away and then hurried down the stairs and back to his truck, back to his bungalow, where he had barely slept. *He was an idiot.*

"Hey, Jake. Wait up."

He glanced over his shoulder to see Trent jogging across the road from the side street leading up to where he and his wife lived at the top of the hill.

"Hey. Sorry."

"Man, you were a thousand miles away." Trent fell into stride beside him. "I saw you coming, plowing down the road like a train, lost in thought. What is on your mind, man? You just kept on going and passed me up without a thought."

Jake rammed his hand through his hair, and

slowed. Moving onto the shoulder, he stopped running. He stared out at the ocean below them. It was a beautiful place to jog but right now he saw none of it. All he saw was Sammy Jo's expression when she realized that he had shut down after the kiss.

He took a deep breath and shot a glance at Trent. "I took someone on a date last night."

"Yeah, so what's new about that?" Trent asked.

The thing about jogging with Trent was that normally they didn't talk much. Trent was the quietest of all of his brothers and when they jogged, they jogged. But today Jake realized that he needed him to be a sounding board.

"I mean, I took someone *special* on a date last night."

Trent grinned. "You like someone. As in *like* her?"

"Hey, don't look so shocked and awed. I mean, I'm not a bad person or anything just because I haven't ever found someone special."

"I think this is great. Jake Sinclair is having a serious thought when it comes to a female."

Jake frowned at his brother. "What if I hurt her? What if I'm not ready? She doesn't deserve to get jerked around because it suddenly turns out that I'm no good with long-term relationships."

Trent stared at him as if he had just met somebody he had never met before. His eyes were wide. "Man, you have fallen and fallen hard."

"There is no falling involved here. Not yet. I'm not sure I'm ready for something like that. I'm just worried…" He sighed. "Man, I am so messed up."

Trent's lips twitched. "You're scared."

"Terrified." He had gone off the deep end during the kiss that shook his world. He kept telling himself all night long that it had just been a kiss.

"It sounds like you care for this girl. Chill, and take your time. I'm going to have to meet her because to tie you up in knots like this, she must really be special. Slow down, get to know her and enjoy yourself. You're overreacting. For me, loving Lilly is the best thing that could ever happen to me. Looking forward to our lives together, not separate, gives me peace. Don't rush it, though. But if you care for her, don't be afraid."

He let Trent's quiet words sink in. Maybe he *was* overreacting. It wasn't as if he were about to suddenly declare his undying love for her after a single kiss. She wasn't expecting that and he knew it.

"Okay, thanks for talking me off that ledge."

"I think you've talked me off a few through the years."

"Maybe. That's what brothers are for."

They stared out at the ocean and then, taking a deep breath, Jake started jogging again and Trent fell into step beside him.

"You'll be okay." Trent grinned.

Jake hoped so. He just had to slow down. But moving slow never had been his strong point. But with Sammy Jo, he could do it. Would do it. Because he would not hurt her.

On her way to Windswept Bay Resort for lunch with Jake's sisters, Sammy Jo went by the newspaper and set up her ads. She was having her grand opening on

Monday. She would have been in Windswept Bay for two weeks by then and was eager to open.

Excitement filled her as she walked into the resort. She still couldn't believe her luck that her creations would actually be displayed in the boutique here at the resort. Her grandmother would love the idea. She really missed her. If she were here, she would have talked to her about what had happened between her and Jake the night before. Because she was really confused by how he had acted after they'd kissed. That kiss had rocked her world. And then he'd shut down and shut her out.

Had she done something wrong?

The question plagued her and she didn't have enough experience to know how to read his obvious withdrawal.

She basically never had anything like this happen to her. Inexperience was hard and made her feel vulnerable. But she was determined to shake it off. She was an adult, after all, and would act like one.

And she had a life to live. Whatever was going on with Jake would sort itself out. At least she hoped so.

Standing in the lobby of the resort, she let the worries slide away and smiled. She was here, standing where her grandparents had once stood. Where they fell in love. It was beautiful. It wasn't huge and spectacular, but breezy and welcoming. It had the prettiest artificial palm trees in the lobby and they gave the atrium a unique look. The lobby was long and narrow, decorated in warm golds and green tones. The ambiance had a soothing effect on her rattled nerves.

At the midpoint of the lobby, there was a pretty staircase that wound around and up to the second floor. But the main focal point of the room was the amazing, gorgeous mural of a waterfall by Cali's husband, Grant. There was no mistaking a Grant Ellington mural. The sea creatures came alive and the light and beauty of it was breathtaking. This waterfall made her feel as if she were beneath the water right next to the fish looking up through the surface at the downpour of water.

"Hi, can I help you?" a young woman behind the desk asked, bringing Sammy Jo out of her musings.

She smiled. "Yes, I'm Sammy Jo Lovely and I'm

here to meet with Cali and her sisters."

"I'll let them know you're here, Miss Lovely. You can wait in the lobby if you'd like."

"Thank you. I think I will look closer at that gorgeous mural. It's amazing."

"Yes, it is. Mr. Ellington's a wonderful artist. We're very lucky to have his work here at the resort."

A few moments later, she saw Cali coming down the stairs with three other pretty ladies. They all resembled each other, except one who had dark hair; the others had varying shades of blonde hair.

Cali came straight to her. "Sammy Jo, it's great to have you here. I was really thrilled to see you with my brother last night."

"I was glad to meet you too."

"These are my sisters. This is Shar. Shar's involved in sea turtle rescue and research. Among other things. And this is Jillian and Olivia, who work with me here at the resort."

"I'm excited to meet all of you." Jake had said Cali was his oldest sister and the other three were triplets. Shar just did not look like Jillian and Olivia.

Jillian smiled. "We are eager to meet the woman who seems to have captured our brother's attention."

Shar grinned impishly. "Cali said Jake looked really happy last night."

Sammy Jo tried not to groan. If they'd seen him at the end of their date, they probably wouldn't say he looked happy. "He's a really nice guy."

"Nice," Shar agreed. "He helps me rescue sea turtles all the time. He'd give you the shirt off his back if you needed it and even if you didn't. He's a nice guy all right. He's just not ever been much into relationships. We're hoping he gets the itch to fall in love soon. Do you think you could fall for our brother?"

Sammy Jo blinked in disbelief at the dark-haired beauty. "I, um, I haven't thought about falling in love." That was a lie and she knew it. She'd found herself thinking about it often since arriving in Windswept Bay.

Olivia chuckled. "Don't let Shar scare you. She's our blunt, to-the-point sister."

She was obviously that. Sammy Jo grimaced. "I

kind of figured that out."

Shar laughed. "Hey, I have to have some fun. Come on, let's go to the beach grill and talk about your boutique. I think that is so cool that you create your own designs!"

"Great idea," Cali said and started toward the sliding glass doors at the back of the building.

As they entered the courtyard, Sammy Jo was struck instantly by how pretty it was with its plants and paved walkways. They walked over several small bridges that led over a lagoon. It wove its way through the grounds and there were even two swans swimming gracefully down the lagoon.

She found out that Jillian was in charge of the grounds. And very obviously a master gardener. Olivia was over the marketing and Cali was the head of everything.

Cali laughed when Olivia pointed that out. "I can tell you, it is a joint effort. I just write the checks from the bank account. And I'm very much hoping to write you some checks."

The thought thrilled Sammy Jo.

They took seats at a table on an outdoor patio next to the white sand beach with the sparkling blue water and matching clear sky. Sammy Jo felt herself relax immediately. It was so beautiful here and she was suddenly struck by the realization that this was where she lived. This was actually her home now, this paradise that most people only came to visit for a few days of vacation.

She had taken the risk and picked up and moved here. And she was now making friends here and setting down roots.

A knot formed inside her chest and lodged hard in her throat as she thought back to how small her world had been only a few months ago. She stayed home with her grandparents, went to the grocery store about three miles from their home—everything she'd needed was within five miles and if not, she'd been a big online buyer. Her world had been very small, but now, things were changing. She had a stab of guilt hit her but denied it because she knew her gram wanted this for her and she had done everything in her power for them while they needed her.

She breathed in deeply and accepted the menu as everyone chattered.

"The chicken salad wrap is amazing," Jillian said.

"And I love the fajita wrap." Shar winked. "It has more kick to it."

Olivia added, "Don't let them pressure you. The Mediterranean salad is to die for."

"Everything on the menu is fantastic," Cali said. "The chef is excellent. He's been with us for years."

Even her food horizons had expanded. Sammy Jo could suddenly not stop grinning.

In the end, she ordered the special of the day, which was chicken with the most amazing parmesan topping and a strawberry and spinach salad that they all agreed was a fantastic dish. She agreed wholeheartedly after taking the first bite.

They talked about getting her clothes in the store and she was thrilled to work out a commission for them that would work for both of them. Lunch flew by and she had such a good time. Jake had been so right when he said she would fit in with his sisters. For the first time in a very long time, she felt the hope that she could actually be a part of something. She blinked back a sudden sweep of emotion. It was as if her gram had known this was her place.

Shar grinned as she finished eating. "So, back to Jake. You are Jake's neighbor, and you went to dinner with him. What do you really think about our Jake—other than he's a nice guy? Cali said he was beaming last night when she saw the two of you."

Obviously Shar was tenacious. "Um, he's great. He's been very helpful since I moved in. But it was just dinner."

"Maybe so." Jillian's big green eyes held a speculative twinkle in them. "But you aren't Jake's normal type. Don't get me wrong—we are thrilled with the situation. Something about you enticed him to ask you out. That is a very good and welcomed thing, we think."

"You *do* like him, don't you?" Cali watched Sammy Jo with an expectant look.

Sammy Jo bit her lip as it hit her that Jake's sisters were *matchmaking.*

The idea sent tremors of uncertainty through her.

"Oh, I don't think there's anything special going on between us. He's just being nice." *Better to put the brakes on their curiosity.* After his reaction last night, she was fairly certain that he didn't feel anything special for her. He'd kissed her and realized there was nothing special there and he'd moved on.

"But you like him, right?" Cali asked again, pressing.

How was she supposed to answer that? Surely, they wouldn't run and tell him what she said. But she wasn't certain about anything at the moment. "Of course. What's not to like? He's a great person." Instant remembrances of what a wonderful kisser he was hit her and of how the feel of his arms around her had filled her with emotions that she did not want to think about right now. Too late, she realized she was blushing and all four of his sisters were smiling triumphantly.

"That's what I thought." Shar slapped her hand to table. "You do like him. Good. Because you are perfect for him. You kind of shake him up in a nice way."

What did that mean?

"No, I mean, there's no need thinking that. Your brother and I, we're too different to ever be considered a couple. He's not afraid to try new things. I mean, he was a Navy SEAL, and he's a diver and he does adventurous things like skydiving and rock-climbing. I've never done any of that. He's just offered to help me conquer a few of those mountains and get them off my bucket—" She clamped her mouth shut, realizing she'd blurted out more than she'd planned.

All the sisters were studying her with open curiosity.

"Bucket *list*?" Olivia finished for her.

Shar's eyes widened. "He's helping you with a *bucket list*? How cool. That'll reel him in."

"Reel him in?" Sammy Jo was worried now.

"Don't mind Shar." Jillian patted Sammy Jo's forearm. "It's something new for Jake. But I think it's great that you have a list. I had a list of sorts and Ryan was on it. Him and our sweet baby were all I wanted and now I have both. April is about to be six months old and I can't believe it. So, bucket list's fulfilled are fabulous."

"That's wonderful. You'll have to bring her by the shop one day. I'd love to meet her. I'm thinking of starting a baby line, just a few cute things with the Lovely You logo on it." *There, maybe that would change the subject.*

"I'll do that. I'm just so excited about you being here and opening your shop." Jillian's warm declaration meant so much to Sammy Jo. And thankfully they gave her a break from too many more questions about Jake.

When she finally left, she felt as if she were leaving friends. And that felt really good.

Of course, the sisters' obvious misunderstanding in thinking Jake had taken an extraordinary interest in her was baffling. They would really have been surprised if she'd confided in them about the kiss and then told them how he'd practically run away after that.

She wasn't special to him. No matter how much she wished it were true.

CHAPTER EIGHT

Jake knocked on the back door of Sammy Jo's shop and waited for her to answer. When she opened the door, his pulse instantly jolted. He'd missed her. He'd stayed away for two days, trying to get his head on straight. But today was their scuba diving lesson and he would not stand her up on that. He'd made a commitment. But the truth was he couldn't stay away any longer.

"Hey." He leaned a shoulder against the doorjamb and crossed his arms. He didn't miss that her eyes held a reserve that hadn't been there before. It didn't sit well that he'd put that look there.

"Hey, yourself." She crossed her arms too. "What's up?"

"Are you ready?"

"*For?*" She looked baffled.

"Our dive lesson," he said, slowly. "At the pool."

Her gaze shifted away and then back to him. "Oh, sorry. I've decided that I'm putting the dive on hold for now. You're busy and I have the grand opening on Monday and there are still things to be done. Sorry, I forgot to let you know. But, then, I haven't seen you, so you are off the hook on that."

The small jab hit its mark. He deserved the distance. "I should have come by, true. But we'd made plans, so I just thought we had a date."

She frowned. "No, no date. I'm really too busy. I have some sewing to do."

"But what about your bucket list?" He didn't like the distance she was putting between them—no, that he had put between them. He had done this.

"Look, Jake. It's fine that you've been avoiding me. I never expected you to spend all your extra time helping me. You've been wonderful, and I think that kiss the other night was probably the last bucket list item I'll be doing for a little while. I have business to tend to. And, well, that kiss shook you up and sent you running and I never planned on that happening."

Sammy Jo had grit and that took him by surprise. He looked away from her as she stared him down with cool eyes. "Yes, that sums it up. That kiss…"

"Scared you." Her brows arched.

He really didn't want to admit that to her, but he bit the bullet. "Yeah, it scared me." He straightened and raked a hand through his hair. "But I talked it over with Trent and he told me for a guy like me it was normal and I should just slow things down." *Boy, was he digging himself deeper into a pit or what?*

"I see. And what about what *I* think? Do *I* get a say in what happens in this relationship or do I just sit back and take whatever you dish out?" Her eyes flashed.

"Yes, sure." He *had* messed up.

"Good. Then, I'm saying, I have a grand opening and I'm shelving the bucket list project for now. I'll finish that on my own after I get my shop going. Now, I need to go finish a skirt. Oh, and by the way, your sisters are fantastic. I like them very much."

And then she closed the door and left him staring at it.

He frowned. This was not at all what he'd expected. He started to knock again but pulled his knuckles back from rapping on the door. Instead, he walked back to his dive shop in a daze.

Soft, quiet Sammy Jo had just shut him out.

Now what?

What had she done? Sammy Jo leaned against the door and waited for her heart to stop thundering. She'd thought long and hard about how to handle the situation with Jake and what she'd just done had happened spontaneously. It had just come to her as she stood there looking at him. It felt good to have cut him off instead of him cutting her off. If this relationship was going nowhere, then it was best to nip it in the bud now. She was not going to be toyed with. And after talking to his sisters, she felt as if Jake probably got whatever he wanted out of a relationship. Well, not this time. This was her new life and she was calling the shots.

But he had looked so good. Dear goodness, the man caused her circuits to go crazy every time he came near. But she was determined to ignore all electrical tingles, tickles, and temptations that tried to influence her choices when Jake was around. And she would not think about kissing him again.

It was too risky. She could fall for him—was falling for him. And then what? He wasn't the commitment kind of guy and she would be hurt if she let anything else happen. She had just moved here and there was no way she was going to let herself be miserable because she fell for the guy next door and couldn't have him.

That was not the way to make a new life somewhere work.

She was strong and determined, and she wanted to at least keep Jake as a friend, so knocking off the romantic stuff was imperative.

So, she would end this. She would end it now.

On Monday, the Windswept Bay Chamber of Commerce came out with a red ribbon cutting ceremony and the paper came to take pictures. Cali, Shar, Jillian, and Olivia were there, as were several of their sisters-in-law. She met Lilly, who was an author, and Kelsey the horse trainer, and Jessica the schoolteacher and Kevin, her adorable little boy. Jessica's husband Levi was the chief of police and he was there also. He was very handsome and obviously very in love with Jessica.

Jake's mother came too. Violet Sinclair was beautiful, with long silver hair and kind eyes.

She took Sammy Jo's hands in hers when she met her. "I'm so glad you've made our home your home. My girls tell me your beloved grandmother just passed away recently and that she and your granddad met at our resort. I'm so very sorry for your loss and if there is anything I can do for you, please don't hesitate to ask. Losing someone you love is hard and yet, you've chosen to start over. You are very brave and I admire you."

Sammy Jo was touched. "Thank you. It has been hard. But I feel close to her here. She told me this is where I belong and I think she is right. This place speaks to me."

"Good. Well, we are having a family dinner at the house on Friday and I'd love for you to come. I'll get Jake to bring you. You and Jake are *friends*, I understand."

She hesitated and glanced across the group to where Jake was talking to his brother Trent. "Um, yes, we are. But I wouldn't want to intrude, though." She hadn't actually talked to him since she closed the door in his face. So it was a bit awkward.

As if sensing she was looking at him, he met her gaze and a smile curved the edges of his lips. She looked away, feeling terrible. "Really, I probably shouldn't—"

"Nonsense. It's a madhouse at our family dinners and there is always room for more. Everyone wants to get to know you better, so please come. Jake will bring you out so you don't have to hunt the place down on your own. Besides, I doubt very much that he will mind."

"Well, okay, that would be great." There was really no graceful way to get out of joining them and she really wanted to. If only there wasn't this tension between her and Jake.

"Jake," Violet called and waved him over.

"Yes, Mom? Do you need me?"

"Yes, I've invited Sammy Jo to dinner on Friday night. Would you be a dear and pick her up and bring her out to the house?"

He stared at Sammy Jo and she wanted to cringe.

"Sure. I'd be glad to."

"Good, then it's all set. Now, I need to go inside and see this store of yours."

Sammy Jo watched the elegant lady walk inside her shop. She was speechless. She had just been railroaded. She felt eyes on her and looked to see Jake grinning at her.

"She got us on that, didn't she?"

She scowled at him. "Yes, but you don't have to

pick me up. I'm capable of driving myself."

"Nope. I promised my mom and I don't break a promise, especially one to my mom."

Figures. "I see. Well, that's a good virtue to have."

He laughed. "Relax. You'll have fun. But if it bothers you for me to pick you up, then I understand."

"No, as long as it doesn't bother you." They stared at each other and she could practically hear the seconds ticking off.

He smiled finally. "It doesn't bother me. I'll pick you up at six. Come casual. We may play Frisbee on the beach or have a bonfire. Kevin loves doing that. And you'll get to meet Rosco and Jaco, Kevin's two dogs, and they are big and active."

She relaxed a little. "I love dogs. But I never had one of my own. I'm thinking one day I'm going to get a small one. One to keep me company in my little apartment."

"You should. We have a great shelter here. That's where Jaco came from. He's a growing moose so the shelter was glad someone took him." He laughed and the sound caused her to laugh too.

"Well, maybe when I'm settled in, I might just go down there and get me a little furry friend."

"It will be a lucky dog."

"Thanks."

"It's the truth." His eyes warmed. "Look, I hope we're okay. I know I messed up the other night."

"We're fine. It's just better this way. We're going to be neighbors for a long time. And we just need to be friends."

"Right."

Moments later, everyone gathered behind the red tape and the newspaper photographer snapped a photo of Sammy Jo cutting the red ribbon. It felt exciting and as if she were part of the community. She was beginning to belong and it felt right. It did. She just had to keep Jake at a distance as a friend.

On Friday night, Sammy Jo closed up the shop, and said a prayer of thanks for the wonderful week she'd had. So many people had come to the shop and she'd sold several outfits. Wearing a smile, she walked up her stairs and into her cozy apartment. It had been a good week. She'd stayed fairly busy and had decided she was going to have to hire some part-time help. She was excited to think that her small business had seen a small victory.

And now she was going to have dinner with new friends. It was a little overwhelming for someone who had as little social life as she'd had for so long. She wanted to make the right impression. She hurried into her tiny bathroom and washed her face and combed her hair. She applied a small amount of makeup and nodded at her reflection in the mirror. "You look fine," she told herself. "Take a deep breath and enjoy yourself." She thought about Jake and knew that was going to be easier said than done.

Her stomach fluttered. She went into her room and opened her closet to go through her clothes. *Casual.* She decided her skirts wouldn't work if they played Frisbee. She'd never played Frisbee. But she had seen people jumping and stretching and catching and throwing the disk before. She opted for a pair of skinny jeans and flip-flops and one of her seafoam tops. She took a deep breath as she walked back into the kitchen and poured herself a glass of water. The knock on the door had her heart instantly racing.

She'd told herself all week not to overreact about spending time with Jake tonight. *It wasn't as if he had asked her out. His mother had set this up. He was just her ride.*

"Just my ride," she muttered as she swung open the door and found him standing there looking better than any man had a right to look. He had a tight, faded T-shirt on with the logo of Jake's Dive Shop on his heart.

He blinked hard as his gaze took her in. "Hi. You look lovely, Miss Lovely. You ready to go?"

"Thank you." She felt like the butterflies erupting in her stomach were having a nervous breakdown. She forced her voice to sound bright and under control. "Let me grab my purse and I'm ready."

She hurried to grab her purse while telling herself to pull her heart back, to hide it somehow. Bury it. Really, it was as if Jake just made her lose her mind when he was near. She had to keep her distance.

She had to.

Moments later, they were driving down the coastal road out of town. "So, you have a very big family. It was so sweet of them to come out to my grand opening and they all bought something. Which they did *not* have to do."

He looked baffled. "Your stuff is gorgeous. Of course they all bought something. You should advertise to husbands and boyfriends and you'll make a mint."

He had a good idea. "Look at you, Mr. Marketer Extraordinaire. That is a very good idea."

His blue eyes twinkled and she couldn't look away. "It just makes sense to me. Did you have a good week?"

"I did. I really did. I love it here. It's as if my gram knew I would."

He shot her a smile, his eyes warm. "Your gram knew you really well. She probably did know you would enjoy it here. I'm really glad she sent you to Windswept Bay."

His words settled in her like warm honey. She fought to keep her feet on the ground. "Even with all the trouble I've been?"

"You're no trouble. Here we are." He drove into a circle drive of a rambling home with beautiful landscaping. There were cars and Jeeps everywhere.

"This yard is so pretty."

"There are so many vehicles it's hard to see the landscaping but my mom and Jillian have very green thumbs, fingers, and toes. They designed the yard. Jillian does it at the resort too."

"Yes, they told me that. I forgot. I don't have a green anything."

"But you can certainly sew."

"True. Maybe one day, when I decide to buy myself a small place, I could talk Jillian into giving me some pointers."

"She would. She's a sweetheart. And wait till you meet little April." The warmth in his words was unmistakable.

"You sound like you enjoy children. You talk about Kevin in the sweetest way and now April. I'm sure you're a great uncle." She studied him as he put the truck into park. *Keep your distance, Sammy Jo.*

"I try to be. I love kids."

Of course, he did. She knew he might not realize it yet but he would make a great father.

"Do you love kids?" he asked.

She nodded. Her heart caught at the thought of being a mom and holding her own baby in her arms. "I do. I want several—not anytime soon. But one day." She had to remind herself not to rush her life. Things would come in their own time. Despite the fact that her life had seemed to be on hold for so long.

He studied her with gentle eyes. "You'll be a wonderful mother."

She fought a sudden lump in her throat. "Thank you. I know that I will love my children with all my heart." She would give her children what her own mother hadn't been able to give her.

"Yes, and they'll be blessed to have you as their mother." He cleared his throat and she tried to breathe as every piece of her soul seemed to want to reach out and cling to him.

"I guess we better go in," he said. But didn't move. They stared at each other.

She managed to nod. "Yes, that would probably be wise." She grasped the door handle and pushed her door open and scrambled from the truck. If she didn't get out of there that she might very well have launched herself at Jake.

He stopped a foot in front of her and placed his hands on his lean hips. "No kidding, Sammy Jo. You will be the best mother."

She could not move. She was in so much trouble because there was no way she was not going to fall in love with this man.

You are not going to fall in love with him. You are not.

She just had to keep repeating the mantra.

CHAPTER NINE

With knots in his stomach, Jake watched Sammy Jo laughing with the crowd of women who now made up the Sinclair women. They were all admiring baby April and looking as happy as could be. It was amazing how they all just clicked. Sammy Jo looked happy and he felt good for her. She had lived such a solitary life and he knew how much making friends and fitting in meant to her. She hadn't even had to tell him that. He had read it in her expressions when she talked about moving here and starting a new life. And when she talked about his family too. She'd just lost everyone who meant anything to her. His heart ached for her. And when she smiled, it made his heart happy. It was a feeling he found he relished.

"You are really lost in thought." Trent walked up and leaned against the counter beside him. "You have it bad, brother."

Jake grunted. "Yeah, but look at her. How can I not have it bad, as you say? But she's happy right now, loving being part of a big gaggle of women. I'm not going to do anything to mess that up."

"Mess what up?" Max came up to lean against the counter too. He reached for a chip and dipped it into a bowl of cheese dip.

"Our brother Jake is in love, but he won't admit it."

Max grinned. "I thought I recognized that dreamy gleam in your eyes."

Jake frowned. "Funny, you two."

"You do have the look," Max reiterated. "It's shell shock. I had it. Felt it. But then I realized Kelsey was everything I ever wanted. Ever needed. Had to have. And there was no way I could let her go."

"I can't risk hurting her. She's lost too much already."

"Then, figure it out." Max wasn't one to ramble on. He and Trent were the quietest two Sinclair men in the family and both of them had just given him heartfelt advice.

"Thanks, fellas."

His dad walked past. "Jake, come help me bring in the burgers."

"Sure." He followed his dad out onto the deck that overlooked the ocean down the hill. Kevin was having a blast. He, Jaco and Rosco were romping on the beach with Levi and his brother-in-law BJ. Gage and Grant were leaning against the railing, watching them and talking.

Jake knew his dad had asked him to help for a reason. There were plenty of people standing around to help. He handed Jake the platter.

"How are you doing?" Sam opened the lid to the massive grill and then began scooping up patties with his large spatula and transferring them to the platter. "We haven't seen much of you around here lately."

"I'm staying busy, Dad."

"Finding some time to date, I see." Sam grinned and scooped up another patty. "Your mom really likes that young lady in there. She thinks you really like her too."

"Sammy Jo is special." He was officially feeling the pressure of his family's expectations now.

"Seems nice. She also seems to have a settling effect on you, I think. Your mom had that effect on me. Kind of makes a man take stock of what's important in life."

Jake thought about that. "Maybe so, but Dad, we're just friends."

Sam looked skeptical and paused his patty picking up. "Right. Truth is, that's the best way to start. Let's get these inside. Hey, Grant, call them up from the beach. Burgers are ready."

"Yes, sir. They sure smell good."

Jake followed his dad in and soon the clan was all sharing a loud and happy meal. He took his burger and sat at the table beside Sammy Jo. "You having a good time?"

"Oh, Jake, yes. You have a wonderful family. I'm a little overwhelmed by so many people and all in one immediate family."

"Yeah, they're cool. Someone always has your back, that's for sure."

"Yes, that's a comfort. I sometimes feel alone." She gave a quick smile. "Well, I am alone but I have friends now."

He covered her hand with his. "Yes, you do." They looked at each other for a long moment. Jake couldn't explain what he felt, except that he felt very protective of her.

"I really love your family, Jake. You're very blessed."

Jake nodded. "Yes, I am. It's a big, growing family. And they all love you too." It took everything in him not to tell her that he loved her. "Are you ready to start preparing to go scuba diving again? I know I messed up with the kiss but I want to get back to spending time with you. And we did start getting you ready to mark that off your bucket list."

She bit her lip. She leaned close. "Jake, this could

blow up in our faces. You were scared after you kissed me the other night. And, well, I'm scared too. I'm scared I could fall for you and you aren't the marrying type. Then what? We work next door to each other and I'd be miserable. And I'm not okay with that. I'm happy here and I don't want to make a huge mistake."

He wanted to pull her into his arms and tell her he'd never hurt her. But she was right. This could go bad. "I messed up the other night. And I can't promise you I won't mess up again, but I will do everything in my power not to hurt you. How do we know if we don't take a risk?"

She inhaled deeply and her green eyes shadowed. "I'm scared," she repeated.

It took everything in him to keep his voice low, to hold back. "You came here to step out and become, in some ways, a risk taker. Take a risk on me."

"What are you two huddled up about?" Shar called from where she and Gage were cuddled on the couch.

Sammy Jo jumped back.

Jake didn't answer his sister but instead hitched a brow at Sammy Jo. "Are we going?"

She held his gaze then nodded.

"Sammy Jo has just agreed to tackle scuba diving. We start lessons tomorrow."

"Awesome, that's great," Shar called. "Jake will get you into all kinds of adventures. I'm a snorkel gal myself, but that's cool. You two are looking good. Hey, Jake, you should bring Sammy Jo to the Windswept Bay Fudge Fest next week."

"Yes, you should," Olivia agreed and then all the females in the room joined in urging him to take Sammy Jo to the Fudge Fest.

Jake couldn't help himself. He tugged gently on a strand of Sammy Jo's silky hair. "Sammy Jo would make anyone look good. And if she wants to go to the Fudge Fest, I'm all in."

Sammy Jo blushed and he wanted to not be sitting in the middle of his parents' home with all of his sisters and brothers and family watching them like hawks. He wanted to be alone with Sammy Jo.

"Do you like fudge?"

"Who doesn't like fudge?"

"Then it's all set. Fudge Fest is next weekend."

"See, that wasn't hard," Shar teased. "You must be losing your touch, brother, if I had to remind you to ask Sammy Jo on a date."

His sister winked and Sammy Jo laughed. Jake's mind wasn't working correctly and that was no lie. But he hadn't liked not getting to spend time with Sammy Jo. And he was hoping she felt the same way about him.

"So, you're crazy about him, right?" Roxie asked over the phone the next day after Sammy Jo had gone to the Sinclair's for dinner.

"Roxie, I am in so much trouble. I'm crazy about him and keep trying to not be. But he's kind of hard to ignore. He talked me into getting back to preparing to go scuba diving. But, Roxie, that's part of the problem. I can get in the pool and I actually managed to go underwater wearing the oxygen mask and breathe in and out without panicking. But the thought of jumping into the ocean and going under terrifies me. He *loves* it. What's he going to think when he realizes I can't do it?"

"Stop being negative. You do not know that you can't do it. And he sounds like he will help you. Don't give up on it right now. Just have fun."

Yeah, sure. It just wasn't that easy. She hung up a few minutes later when customers entered the shop to browse.

By the time she locked the front door and went up to her apartment to change, excitement over seeing Jake again helped push back the worry over the scuba diving. If she hadn't promised Gram she would try it, Sammy Jo knew she would delete it from her bucket list. But she had promised.

She pulled on shorts over her swimsuit and slipped her feet into her sandals. She buttoned the front of her blouse over her swimsuit and then, grabbing her purse, she headed back down the stairs to wait for Jake. He would think she was eager to get to their class but the truth was she was just eager to see him.

"I thought this day would never end," he said when he met her at the foot of the stairs.

As she looked at him, every worry that she'd had

all day melted away. "Me too." She had missed him.

When they reached the pool, she felt as though she had a heavy case of indigestion. Despite the indigestion, she was distracted thinking about being near Jake. He was so distracting with his muscles and Adonis looks and those blasted twinkling eyes that were full of mischief and life. She loved that about him. How alive he was.

If just some small amount of that could rub off on her, then her life would be far more adventurous than ever before.

"Okay, so we'll practice breathing with the regulator and several other skills you'll need. Then next week, we'll get you out on an actual dive."

A knot of indigestion tried to kink up behind her sternum. "Sure. Perfect."

He helped her strap on the air tanks and she was aware of every time he touched her. She concentrated on that feeling instead of the dread that she was getting one step closer to marking off the major hurdle on her bucket list. Her and Gram's bucket list. Gram had wanted to scuba dive so badly. She remembered listening to Gram talk about how much she regretted never learning. That when she and Granddad had first met, he had urged her to learn and go with him but fear had held her back. She regretted that the rest of her life.

Memories are worth the effort. That's what Gram had said over and over. Working hard to make memories, not regrets, was worth pushing and stretching yourself.

And so, scuba diving had gone on the bucket list. Despite her claustrophobia and fear of suffocating, Sammy Jo had told herself that she would make the dive.

But the problem was that she just might not make it.

She might not have gumption enough, as her gram called it, to get that particular item marked off her list.

And if she couldn't mark it off, that would be one of, if not the greatest, regret of her life.

Jake was having a hard time concentrating on scuba

diving readiness. The minute he picked Sammy Jo up, he felt as if he'd been kicked in the lungs by a mule and he was struggling to breathe ever since. The woman took his breath away. But as they moved into the pool, he had the feeling that something was bothering her.

The other time that they'd practiced with the oxygen tanks, he had thought she was nervous. She struggled a little to actually go under the water and breathe through the regulator. He knew that some people had trouble with that technique.

"Hey, so take it easy. Let's work on your breathing and getting comfortable with using the regulator. You seem a little nervous."

"It's not exactly a natural process. It does rattle me a little."

"No problem. We'll go slow."

"Okay. I'm all for that."

Later, after she submerged under the water and he worked with her on using her equipment while submerged, he felt better about her responses. When they headed back to the apartment, she was more relaxed. He was too, because being so near Sammy Jo had him wound up and struggling to keep his hands to himself and his concentration on anything other than the fact that she was adorable. More than adorable. She was mind-bogglingly distracting. He was having a hard time these days thinking about anything but her.

He knew there was no denying how he felt for her. He'd fallen, and fallen hard, in love with her. And he couldn't run from it.

Truth was he'd been feeling that way for a while.

"So, that was fun," he said as they reached the steps that led up to her apartment.

"Yes, it was. It's still got me a little uptight but I'm working on it. Thanks for being patient. What's up with the Fudge Fest? I need to call Shar and find out if I need to have something in the festival. I mean, do vendors have booths? Or is it mostly a food thing?"

"Some people have booths. But mostly it's food related. We are in a tourist town. Fudge is a big part of tourist towns. I'm not really sure, because it's not like I go on trips and eat a lot of the rich stuff. But obviously many people do because the fudge shops in town do great business. I think Grant may have some art pieces in an auction that is going to charity. That should be fun."

"It sounds like it. Thank you for taking me."

"I'm just sorry my sister beat me to asking you out. I would have asked you that night but Shar and her big mouth decided to butt in and ask you for me."

Sammy Jo giggled. "Your family does seem to think they need to do the asking for you. Why is that?"

"The truth?"

She nodded and leaned against the stair railing with her hands behind her back as she studied him. He wanted to lean in and kiss her.

"They are afraid I'll miss how great you are and mess up. They are trying to ensure that I give us time to get to know each other. And then there is the fear part. They are afraid that I will get cold feet and back down and shut down."

"Oh. Do you think you would?"

He stepped close. She stood on the bottom step, bringing them to the same height. He placed his hands on either side of her on the railing and stared deeply into her beautiful green eyes. "I did the other night. But no more. I had never felt what I was feeling before and it scared me. But I think I'm way over that." She inhaled deeply, drawing his gaze to her lips. "What about you, Sammy Jo? Are you scared?"

He leaned close, and her jeweled-toned eyes flashed wide. "N-no. Not scared," she said, breathless.

His lips curved upward. "Good." And then he gave in to the overwhelming desire he was feeling. He kissed her. She froze as his lips touched hers. He paused, letting his lips press against hers and feel the slight tremble that vibrated beneath his. And then he scooped one arm behind her and pressed his hand against the small of her back as he fully captured her lips with his. This was right.

This was home.

When Sammy Jo's hands came to rest against his shoulders, every cell in his body tensed.

"Jake," she breathed against his lips. "What are we doing?"

"We're enjoying ourselves."

"But," she said, breathless. "What if it doesn't

work out?"

He didn't want to scare her away with too much too soon. "What if it does? Stop worrying. Jump. I'm tired of worrying and want to explore what is between us. I can't resist this."

He pulled her into his arms and let himself explore every wonderful feeling that exploded through him as their mouths melded together. He wasn't sure he would be able to stop.

And knew he didn't ever *want* to stop.

What was she doing? Sammy Jo's heart pounded erratically as she clutched two fistfuls of his shirt and kissed him like there was no tomorrow. Tomorrow she might be rational again. But tonight, she was taking a risk. She was jumping. She was all in.

And with the way his lips felt on hers, and the churning, burning desire pulsing through her, she wasn't real sure she would ever let this kiss end.

After what seemed like too soon, he pulled away and let their foreheads rest against each other as they both fought to regain control of their breathing.

"Well, I'm really surprised I'm still standing. You melt my knees and my heart, Sammy Jo."

"And you did the same to me, Mr. Sinclair. That was some kiss."

"I liked it," he said in a deep, raspy growl. "I'm not sure I can move away from you."

She chuckled. "Good, because I'm not sure I can let go of you."

"Then we'll just stand here looking out at that moonlit water while we regain control."

And that was exactly what they did.

CHAPTER TEN

Sammy Jo had thrown caution to the wind and kissed Jake until she was breathless and unable to think straight. It was a feeling that she could get used to. She could kiss Jake forever. But when he found out just how much of a fake she was, there was no way he could kiss her forever. She could never hold onto a man like him.

The thought filled her mind and she tried not to think about the depressing thoughts the next few days. Of course, she would be working and, out of the blue, his kiss would steal into her thoughts and she'd find herself just staring off into nothing with a goofy grin on her face.

Like now. A shiver of awareness hit her as the bell on the door jangled and she shook herself out of her kissing thoughts. It was Jake's sister, Olivia.

Olivia swept into the shop, looking gorgeous in a green sundress. "I was driving by and wondered if you had time to come to lunch?"

Sammy Jo's day brightened instantly. "Sure, I'd love it. Now?"

Olivia chuckled. "Yes, now. We're actually all heading to Lilly's treehouse. Lilly is all excited because she just finished a new book and she's itching to celebrate. The girl holes up during the writing of the books and sometimes we see her and sometimes we don't. At the dinner the other night, I don't know if you noticed, but she was a little distracted. That's because she was nearing the end of her book but Trent had practically kidnapped her and brought her to Mom's to eat. He says he's barely seen her since. But she finished yesterday and called to have us all come out to celebrate."

"That sounds great. Let me grab my bag. It's kind of dead today anyway. I really need to hire some help, though, so I'm not always tied down to the shop."

"Yes, or we'll be accusing you of being a recluse."

They locked up and she slid into the passenger's seat of Olivia's sports car. "So, Lilly and Trent live in a treehouse?"

Olivia's green eyes sparkled. "Yes, they do. Actually, they have two houses. The treehouse is really her writing get-away. It's pretty awesome."

They were driving down the ocean drive and after just a little distance outside the city limits, she turned onto a road that wound upward.

"This is the tallest area of Windswept Bay. You can see for miles." Olivia drove her little car around the curving road until they came to a turnaround with a private gate. She pushed a button and in a moment, the gate opened and they pulled through. Once inside, there were other cars lined up beneath the canopy of trees.

"It is really cool up here." She was intrigued.

"Yes, just wait. Trent is a very talented guy. And

he created Lilly's vision perfectly."

They walked through the trees and stepped up onto a boardwalk that rose from the ground and wove through the trees. She gasped when she saw the actual treehouse through the thick trees with the boardwalk stairs leading up to it. She could see all the other Sinclair women milling around on the deck.

Shar waved and so did Jillian. Excitement swam through Sammy Jo.

"I am so glad you came," Lilly said the moment they stepped onto the deck. "Welcome to my treehouse."

"I love it. I wouldn't have missed seeing this for all the world." She turned and looked out over the treetops to the ocean in the distance. "This is amazing. And you write up here?"

"I do. Gets my creative juices flowing. But it's not healthy for me to shut out the world, so my new deal is that when I finish a book, I celebrate with all my new sisters."

Her words sank in and Sammy Jo felt like an impostor again. *Did they all just automatically assume that she and Jake were together? Was Lilly including her in the sisters description because she thought there was more between her and Jake than there was?*

Suddenly she felt very uncomfortable about misleading her new friends. *Would they all still want her around when Jake moved on to someone who fit him better?*

The idea sat like a lump in the pit of her stomach. She had decided she might be getting an ulcer worrying about being an impostor.

"Okay, I'm ready." Shar came out of the treehouse wearing a harness around her hips and a little red helmet. The dark-haired beauty's eyes were gleaming as she rubbed her hands together. "I tell you, my brother is a genius and every time I come out here, I'm more and more convinced that I need to have him make me a zipline somewhere on mine and Gage's property. Why should you be the only one who gets to have fun on a whim?"

Lilly laughed. "He'd build you one. You know he would. He'd build you a treehouse, too, if you wanted one. He loves building them."

Sammy Jo looked on, totally confused. She watched as Shar walked over to the stairs that led up to the second-story deck. They'd told her that that was actually Lilly's writing room. And it was then that she noticed a platform and a wire. A wire with a handle and a connector on it. "What is that?" she asked.

Cali smiled from where she was leaning against the deck railing, looking out at the view. "That is Lilly's zipline. Trent's love for treehouses extends to adult-sized surprises that would make a kid's mouth water."

Sammy Jo's stomach dropped to her toes and bounced. "Shar is going to ride down that?"

She stared at the wire that she now saw ran through the trees and wove around and eventually ended near the ground. It was one of the scariest things she'd ever looked at. And yet it was also intriguing. And Shar looked exhilarated as she stepped up onto the platform and hooked herself to the heavy-duty line.

"Yes, it is the most fun. We've all done it. We love coming out here and riding down." Cali was an elegant beauty with a class that Sammy Jo could never hope to have. Imagining Cali riding down that zipline was about as out of character for Cali as Sammy Jo could imagine.

"You ride that thing?"

Cali winked. "Yes, and while I'm not as crazy about it as my zealous sister, Shar or sis-in-law, Lilly, I really enjoy it. It kind of clears your head and makes you feel like a kid again. You should do it. It's very safe."

Something in Sammy Jo twisted. As she held her breath, she watched Shar position her helmet more securely and then, grinning, she waved.

"Okay, kiddos, I'll be right back!" And then with a squeal of pure joy, Shar pushed off the edge of the platform and, holding onto the handlebars, sailed out into nothingness.

Sammy Jo gasped. Her stomach rolled and she watched Shar with envy as she flew through the trees, laughing with glee. She even let go of the handlebars and leaned back with her arms held wide open. Sammy Jo had a sudden, overwhelming desire to let go like that. To live, without fear.

"You would enjoy it," Jillian said softly, coming to stand beside her. "Really, why don't you do it?"

"Yes." Kelsey smiled. "I enjoy keeping my feet firmly in the stirrups of my horses saddles, but that zipline is addictive. I'm going next, unless you want to go. I'll wait until after you go to do it."

"Me? I don't know. I don't know if I could—"

Lilly studied her. "You can do it. It's scary until you take the first leap, and then you never look back. Come on, let's get you into a harness."

"Oh, no, I couldn't," she stammered. But the next thing she knew, she was surrounded by Sinclair women and they were all encouraging her. She was really embarrassed about trying to weasel out of it. They would all think she was a big chicken. And before she could get enough objections out, Shar was back and all of her new friends had practically coerced her into getting up on the platform wearing a helmet and a harness.

She was about to kill herself. As sure as she was a female coward, she was about to see her last sunset as she plummeted to her death through the canopy of these beautiful trees. And all of her so-called new friends were going to be cheering on from the treehouse.

How had this happened? The question rolled over her like a steamroller. She was sweating and feeling faint. "Really, I don't know if I can do this."

"You can do this. I think you need to do this," Shar said, mischief in her eyes. "Want me to push you?"

"*Push me?*" she asked, startled that Shar would even suggest that she just give her a shove off the platform. She was holding onto the handlebars with a death grip. It was her last shot to get off the platform. She needed to just back off the platform and take the harness off. But somehow, she was still standing on the platform, knees knocking and stomach curdling.

Had she lost her ever-lovin'-mind?

In the next instant, she didn't have time to ask herself this question, because Shar misunderstood when she'd said "Push me?" Shar thought she was actually telling her to actually push her.

And Shar did exactly that.

One minute, Sammy Jo was standing on the platform with her knees knocking together like bongos and then suddenly hands shoved her in the back and sent her sailing out into the air.

"What!" she screamed as her weight caused the wire to dip downward. She screamed again, clutched the handlebars with a death grip as her feet swung free beneath her and her scream died in her throat when she realized she was not falling but flying. Gliding like greased lightning through the trees, a feeling of freedom and wonder.

CHAPTER ELEVEN

"Are you fudged out yet?" Jake asked her a few nights later as they wandered along the main street that the Fudge Fest was set up on. The delicious scent of fudge filled the air and it was about as sweet as it could get.

"I think I'll pop if I try to eat any more. It is wonderful, though."

He grinned. "Yeah, it is. I'm pretty much done too. How about a cup of coffee?"

"That sounds wonderful. Something to take the sweet edge off."

He led the way over to a booth that was serving all types of drinks, coffee included. "I'm still trying to wrap my mind around the fact that you did the zipline at Lilly and Trent's place. I wish I had been there."

Sammy Jo beamed. "I loved it. I mean, like I told you, I was terrified. Really, really terrified. But your sister Shar, crazy woman, she shoved me off that platform without hesitation. If I could have jumped back on the platform, I probably would have strangled her, but of course I couldn't. And after the initial lose-my-stomach moment, the exhilaration took over and it was amazing. I get chill bumps every time I think about it."

He grinned at her. "I should have warned you not to turn your back on Shar. She's something else."

"Yes, in a very good way. Oh Jake, I just feel amazing." They got their coffee and walked out to a bench and sat down. "I can't imagine not living here in Windswept Bay."

He couldn't imagine her not being here either. Looking at her, he had the overwhelming need to pull her into his arms and ask her some very important questions.

But those questions…struck fear in him. *Was he cut out for life as a married man? Would committing himself to being a family man last for him?*

He'd always held onto the knowledge that all he had to take care of in life was himself. No one really relied on him. He'd had men depending on him when he'd been in special ops, and after he'd gotten out, he'd just never been able to hold someone else's fate in his hands. *Could he commit?*

His brothers all seemed to love their new lives as family men. He envied them and yet when it came down to actually saying the words of love and commitment to Sammy Jo, he clammed up.

And so he just smiled. "You fit in perfectly. I'm glad you're enjoying it. You ready to take that first dive next week?"

She froze with her coffee midway to her lips. Her eyes widened and he thought he saw panic. Then her jaw tensed and she nodded. "Let's do this. If I can jump out of a treehouse connected to a cable, then surely I can dive into the ocean with an air tank."

On Sunday, with her nerves tangled together, Sammy Jo met Jake on the dock. She was nervous but feeling better about herself since Shar had pushed her off the zipline. She could give herself a shove on getting this dive done and off her bucket list. Her gram would be proud of her.

"You ready to get this done?" Jake grinned at her with a sparkling smile and twinkling eyes as he took her hand and steadied her as she stepped into the boat. He didn't step back but instead remained where he was, which brought them chest to chest. Her insides got all shaky and gooey and she wanted to throw herself into his arms. She had it bad and there was no getting past it.

"I am," she said, breathless. Her pulse raced as she looked up into his eyes. "I'm a little nervous, though." She was nervous—on all kinds of levels.

He lifted his hand and caressed her cheek. "Sammy Jo, you don't have anything to be nervous about. I wouldn't ever let anything happen to you. I'm crazy about you. Really, really crazy about you."

Shivers raced down her spine. She told herself not to let his affection go to her heart. *Do not let him get to my heart.* She told herself to remember the way he'd pulled back after their kiss on the moonlit beach. There was no guarantee that he wouldn't do that again, despite the fact that he'd apologized several times.

Would he pull back again? Could she trust him?

They had been having a good time since the night at his parents' home. She reminded herself that that hadn't been a date. His mother had set that up by asking him to pick her up. But she hadn't been able to get the lovely evening off her mind. It had felt so good to feel as if she belonged. It was a feeling she did not need to let herself get too connected to. At least not as someone special to Jake. But then he'd talked her into dive lessons again and they'd gone to the Fudge Fest together and the days had just rolled comfortably into each other.

And now, the feel of his hands against her jaw was doing funny things to her thought process as she stared into his eyes. *He was crazy about her. Did crazy about her equate to love her?* The question echoed through her.

"You…what?" she mumbled, managing to speak past the thoughts jumbling through her.

He smiled. "I will never let anything happen to you. Trust me."

She was mesmerized by his eyes and realized they were still staring at each other.

Trust. It was a hard word. "Okay, great. I will," she managed.

"Good. We better get going. We have a bucket list wish to mark off." He backed up and gave her room to move into the boat.

Within minutes, they were racing across the bay. She thought about how Jake was acting all the way to the dive spot. He had almost acted as if he cared for her, as more than a friend. She knew she cared for him. She had tried and tried to deny it but she couldn't any longer. But she was scared that he was not a commitment kind of guy. So, it wasn't very smart of her to fall for him. But as they rode the waves and the sea spray hit her and the salt air filled her lungs, clearing her mind, she knew…she loved Jake Sinclair. She had let him get past her barriers.

She suddenly felt sick. *Now what?*

When they reached the dive spot, Jake helped her slip into her wet suit and they went through all the procedures he had taught her in their times at the pool. The closer it came to actually going into the water, the more her blood pressure rose. She kept practicing her breathing and told herself that if she could breathe through the regulator in the pool, she could do it in the ocean.

And Jake was going to be right there with her.

He frowned, a goal post of concern etched between his eyebrows. "Are you okay? You look like you feel bad."

She took a shaky breath. "I'm fine. Well, okay, the closer it comes to actually getting in that water and going down there with only my air coming from this tank strapped to my back, the more nervous I get.

Panicked, actually."

She could be a risk taker. No, she had never really taken a risk—jumping off the platform of the zipline hadn't actually been her taking a risk. It had been Shar shoving her into it.

Her mouth was dry.

This was pretty risky, no matter what Jake said. He was a Navy SEAL, after all. There was nothing that scared him. Her…well, this actually scared her.

"I'm scared actually," she admitted because she basically couldn't deny it any longer. *This was it.* Truth time.

His frown deepened. "You do know you don't have to do this if you don't want to. I won't feel any differently about you. There is no shame in not enjoying something."

Tears pricked at her eyes. "But Jake, I'm a wimp. Do you know how much I hate being a wimp? When I put it on my list, I was feeling all brave and determined. And Gram was all proud because she was feeling that way too. Scuba diving seemed like such a cool thing to challenge myself to do. So, Gram urged me to put it on the list because she always regretted not doing it."

"Okay, so here is the thing—I've been meaning to ask you what parts of this list were you and what parts were your gram. What on this list do *you* want to do?"

Her brows scrunched. "Well, the dive is mostly Gram. But I want to be brave enough."

"But that just doesn't seem like the thing that a bucket list should be about. Shouldn't it be about things you enjoy and long to do? Why don't you step back and think about this? There are a lot of things that could be on your bucket list that maybe will challenge you, but also that you would enjoy. I just wonder about having to force yourself to do this."

"But you love it."

"So? It's my passion. Don't you get that? It's *my* passion. I would never want you to do something that you are uncomfortable with."

She swallowed hard. "But I feel like I failed."

He tugged her against him. "You didn't fail. It's your choice what you want to do. You enjoyed snorkeling the other day." He leaned back and looked into her eyes. "And that wasn't even on your bucket list. What if you just trade that out with this dive?"

She couldn't believe he was so calm about this. She sank down onto the bench seat. Her knees felt weak. *This was why she wasn't right for Jake.*

The knowledge sank in. He deserved someone braver, full of fun and a risk taker. And she just wasn't. And she'd known it all along.

He sat beside her. The boat rocked as she stared out across the beautiful topaz water surrounding them. "I love looking at this water. I loved snorkeling because I was above the water, looking down. But the truth is, I'm claustrophobic and it took every ounce of effort I had to go underwater in the pool with the regulator on. But to think about being below the surface of that big, beautiful ocean overwhelms me."

"You should have been honest with me. I'm not used to taking people diving who don't really want to do it. Let's get that outfit off you and let's go do something you'll enjoy. And then, I think you need to look over your bucket list and turn it into what you want. Your gram loved you, and I am pretty sure she wouldn't want you to do anything you don't want to do."

Feeling completely defeated, she sighed and gave in. She wanted to cry all the way back to the dock. Because she knew in her heart of hearts that Jake Sinclair deserved someone he could live life to the fullest with. And that was not the likes of her. And that broke her heart.

He needed more than a scared, wimpy gal who couldn't keep up with him.

Jake worried about Sammy Jo all the way back to the boat dock. He had thought something about the dive was bothering her, but he hadn't picked up on the fact that she really didn't want to do it. Now, he knew she was being hard on herself.

As soon as he docked the boat, he cut the engine and looked at her. "Okay, now, we have an entire afternoon to do something fun."

She looked really sad. Defeated even.

"I don't know. I think I'll just go to my apartment

and do some work."

He stared at her. "Nope. Trust me. There is more to do that's fun that has nothing to do with extreme sports. And guess what? I enjoy those things too. Come hiking with me. I'd love to show you something beautiful."

She took a deep breath and looked interested. "I don't know."

"You were supposed to spend the afternoon with me. Don't let me down. I was counting on it."

She sighed. "Okay, but you are not playing fair."

"Maybe not, but all I'm interested in right now is doing whatever I have to in order to spend time with you. You might want to run up and grab some sturdier shoes instead of those flip-flops. I'll wait here for you."

"Okay. I'll be right back."

She jogged up the stairs and he watched her go. His heart was pounding. He was crazy about her. And he had realized that he didn't want to lose her.

She came back down wearing running shoes and a smile. "Ready. I'm feeling better. I can't wait to see what you want to show me."

"Then let's go. Your chariot awaits you."

Sammy Jo had given herself a pep talk as she'd put her shoes on and now, as she followed Jake up a hillside, she kept trying to convince herself that everything wasn't as bad as she thought. But she knew it was. She could never hope to hold a man like Jake. He would need a woman who wasn't afraid to jump into the ocean and explore the worlds beneath the surface with him. He would need a partner in life who could keep up with him. And she might as well resolve herself to that fact and learn to live with it. Windswept Bay had everything she could possibly ever want or desire. Except an inner braveness that only she could muster up. She'd risked everything by letting herself fall in love with Jake.

Risked it all and lost.

And now, she just had to be a graceful loser and try not to let him see just how much she cared for him. If she could hide her feelings, then he wouldn't feel so bad when he finally found his soul mate.

The best thing she could do was let him go. *Just be friends.*

And love him at a distance.

She would be the quintessential girl next door. The friend and never the lover.

Never the loved.

By the time they reached the waterfall, she had become quite depressed. She should have stayed home.

But when they walked through the trees, suddenly the forest opened up and there in front of them was the waterfall cascading down the rocks and splashing in the green pool below them.

She gasped. "Oh, oh, Jake. I had no idea this was here. It is breathtaking."

He turned toward her and smiled. "Just like you."

His words filled her and caused her to take a shaky breath. He was so very sweet.

"A little more exciting than me. But wow, just wow."

He took her hands. "Actually, I disagree. You see, this waterfall is very much like you. See, that first day when I looked up and saw you standing in the doorway of your shop, you took my breath away. I couldn't take my eyes off you. I could come to this waterfall and look at it all day long and never grow tired of it. It bubbles with life and hope and beauty. And so do you. And it doesn't have to do anything to make me love it more than what it already does. It draws me to it. It infatuates me and it makes me stand here and take in my surroundings and fills me with peace. That's what you do to me. But it's your heart and your selfless spirit that draws me to you the most."

She blinked back tears. His words started to sink in. "But you are so full of life. You need a woman who can keep up with you."

He cupped her face in his hands. "I need a woman who balances me out and fills me with peace, love, and joy. That's you, Sammy Jo 'So' Lovely. I know you feel bad about the dive. But I personally couldn't care less about that. You can leave it as a goal if you want and we will spend the rest of our lives seeking to achieve it. Or who knows, you could do it next week. Me, I don't care. I want to make a new bucket list that you and I want to fulfill together. And the top of that list is I want you to become Mrs. Jake Sinclair. I want you to be my wife. If I remember correctly, there is one other thing on that bucket list that my wish would complete if you felt the same way and said yes."

Her breath caught. And tears welled in her eyes. *She wanted to fall in love.* That was the last item on her bucket list and the most important item on the list.

And she had fallen in love. *But could she take the risk that she could hold a man like him?* "But are you sure?"

"Trust me, I've never been more certain about anything than that I love you. I'd say take a risk on me. But to be honest, where my heart is concerned, there is no risk. It's yours forever if you love me too."

She inhaled. Her heart swelled and tears trailed down her cheeks. "I love you, Jake Sinclair. And I want to create a bucket list with you."

He let out a whoop and scooped her into his arms. "Let's start with a kiss and build from there."

His lips covered hers and she twined her arms around his neck and held on tightly. She'd taken a risk to come to Windswept Bay and now, all of her dreams were coming true.

And she had a feeling her gram was marking the last item off her list, knowing that Sammy Jo had found Jake on the shores of Windswept Bay.

Which was exactly what her gram had wanted.

Excerpt from

WITH THIS VOW

Windswept Bay, Book Eleven

CHAPTER ONE

Moonlight shimmered in the dark room as Cam Sinclair woke to find himself alone in his bed. Unease rustled through him. He immediately sat up, looking around for his wife. Where was Lana?

Getting up, he silently walked down the hallway of their ranch house. The soft light coming from the nursery made it easy to find her. He paused at the doorway. Lana sat in the cushioned rocking chair, gently rocking with her eyes closed, her dark hair cascaded over her shoulders and her body full and round with their baby, she was more beautiful than ever. A tsunami of love washed through him, holding him transfixed by its power. This amazing woman carried their baby girl in her womb and in less than six weeks, they would be parents.

For a man good at being calm and in control, he felt a bit overwhelmed about the idea of being a dad. A worthy responsibility that had settled solidly on his shoulders the moment they'd learned they were expecting. He had more respect than ever for his dad now that he understood what it meant to father a child, and to want with all of his heart to be the best father he could be.

And the best husband.

The baby, named Eva Marie, after Lana's mother, was due the week after Christmas and right now, two days before Thanksgiving, his heart was overwhelmed with gratitude for the blessings in his life.

"Hey, beautiful," he said after a moment. Her eyelids fluttered open, startled but clearing as she watched him cross the room to her. He leaned down to gently kiss her lips, catching the shadows of worry in her eyes. "Is everything okay?" He knew she was struggling to find a balance of emotions right now.

"Everything is wonderful." She cupped his cheek with her hand as her emerald eyes met his.

She had beautiful eyes. The startling color was a Presley genetic masterpiece that, though shared by her dad and all five of her brothers, was still a unique jewel tone all her own and amazing to him with the depth and clarity. And as much as she tried, he could see her struggle.

"This is going to be a busy month," she continued. "I couldn't sleep so I'm rocking Eva Marie and…" Her hand dropped to her stomach.

He knelt at her side and placed his hand over hers, felt it tremble beneath his. There was more to this. "What's really on your mind?"

She sighed. "I'm missing my mother." Her words were softly spoken but seemed to echo in the pink and white decorated room as if it were a dark hollow cavern.

His heart ached for her. "I can only imagine how

much you must miss her, especially during this special time."

His own mother had been a guiding force behind his huge family of four sisters and four brothers. She still was and could hardly wait until next week when he and Lana would make an early Christmas trip home to see his family in Windswept Bay. It would be a short trip before flying back here to Texas to spend the holiday at the ranch, close to Lana's doctors. He wasn't taking any chances and the doctor had assured him that she was okay to fly there and back on the private jet owned by his brother-in-law Gage. As long as they were home three weeks out from the due date.

"I'm sure she's looking down with all her love from above."

"Yes, I know she's with me and I've thought I was at peace with having lost her. But every day this precious baby grows inside me, I ache to share this with her. I have sweet Aunt Trudy, and Sally Ann, and Gert who all stepped in to be there for me as I was growing up in Ransom Creek. They've been like my mother's angels, watching out for me. But still…" Her words trailed off. No words were needed as the deep, aching, heartfelt wish hung in the air, filling the room with emotion.

The worry that had been a low simmer in his gut from the moment they'd learned they were expecting now churned. Lana's mother died giving birth to Lana. The dangers of child birthing were ever-present in their lives considering Eva Presley had died of unexpected complications, which made it more nerve-racking.

Was it something that could be genetic? He pushed the apprehension away, not wanting to let the fear steal the joy of the moment in their lives. The doctors had told them everything was fine. Nothing looked abnormal and he held onto their words.

It was harder for Lana to let go of and he understood. She and her brothers had been brought up by her dad and his sister, Aunt Trudy. Despite the love and closeness of the family, he knew from long conversations with Lana that nothing had ever filled the hole that their mother's loss had left in all of their lives.

Cam couldn't imagine losing Lana. How had Marcus, her father, been able to handle the anguish and pain that he must have felt?

It was unbearable to Cam to even think about it.

He tried hard not to let Lana know his fear but he wouldn't rest easy until the day he brought both his wife and their baby home from the hospital.

Unable to bear it, Cam slipped one arm beneath her knees and then slid his other arm between her back and the rocking chair and scooped her into his arms. He lifted her up as she laughed, startled by his action. He stood there, holding her and his baby, and leaned his head against her forehead; her laughter died and she buried her face against his neck, clinging to him. He breathed in the fresh spring flower-scented soap that she loved. He could hold her forever.

"I love you, Lana. What you're feeling is understandable. What you need is to hold Eva Marie in your arms and you'll give her enough love for you and your mother."

She nodded against his neck. Her arms quivered

and her breath stuttered against his skin as she fought back emotion. "You're right. I'm an emotional wreck right now."

"You're a beautiful mother-to-be."

They stood together for the longest time, him just holding her and then when she relaxed against him, he strode back to their bedroom and gently laid her in the bed. She was exhausted and didn't stir as he crawled in behind her. Drawing her close, he just held her and watched her sleep. His usually strong wife was vulnerable right now.

But everything was going to be all right.

It was. He'd make sure of it.

He just needed to make sure he gave her every ounce of support she needed through this last leg of the pregnancy. And this uneasy feeling in his gut that continued to linger…he'd just rack it up as nerves of a soon-to-be dad.

He was a man who was now responsible for a treasure on earth…responsibility he took with serious intent, so what he was feeling was normal. *Right?*

Maybe so, still, as he watched Lana sleeping, he couldn't shake the feeling that something wasn't right.

The morning after Cam had found her worrying in the baby's nursery, Lana woke feeling as if she'd cried all night. Which she hadn't done. She'd actually fallen asleep in his arms and had woken as he brought her breakfast in bed. The man was amazing. She'd gotten through the surge of emotions that had driven her from bed last night and now she would get through the day. It was a good day. It was the day of her baby shower so they were driving the two hours to Ransom Creek, her hometown, where her friends and family were holding the shower for her. That thought had lifted her spirits.

Now, Lana surveyed the room of dearly loved women who had gathered in the living room of Sally Ann's Junk Shop Bed-and-Breakfast. Lana had always loved the homey, comfortable feel of this place. As a girl growing up without a mother of her own, she'd loved spending time here with her Aunt Trudy. She'd brought Lana here for all types of gatherings that her aunt and her two best friends, Sally Ann and Gert Goodnight, had at least once a week. Girls night, and they'd included Lana when she was growing up.

Her heart tugged watching the three ladies: Sally Ann—tall and still wearing her hair bleached blonde and long, swinging in her ever-present ponytail. Aunt Trudy—plump, shorter, and a ball of energy who loved to get into everyone's business. And then Gert—tiny, matter-of-fact attitude with a heart of gold. She loved each of them and had been silently cheering them on over the last eighteen months as they'd meddled their way through helping all her brothers find love.

And that pleased her. She loved each of their wives. Beth and Cooper were perfect for each other, and Shane and Jenna were a match meant to be. Vance and Libby were adorable together, and Brice and Tara were like two stars colliding every time they looked at each other. And her dad and Karla were blissfully happy since working things out and getting married. Even her best friends, Lori and Trip, had married, and her cousin Carson and Bella. Love was rampant in

Ransom Creek. The only one yet to tie the knot was big brother Drake. Oh, he was in love and had loosened up and was learning to enjoy a more adventurous life now that Maisy Love had come into his life. But they hadn't announced a wedding date yet. Maybe soon.

She was hoping they'd come up with a wedding date soon but she knew they were holding off until she had the baby. They didn't want to schedule the wedding and take the chance of it and the baby's birth competing against each other. Plus, there was Vance and his quest to win the National Finals Rodeo in December. And Maisy had a cooking event in Vegas, too, on that same week.

Lana knew all their reasons for waiting but she was eager for them to tie the knot.

"Okay, little mama." Beth bent over and pinned a baby bootie corsage to Lana's shirt just above her heart. "It's time to get this party started."

Lana looked down at the cute pink and white concoction. "It's adorable."

"I had fun making it for you. And your brother,

he's so romantic, was standing behind my chair, trying to distract me with kisses on my neck asking questions about when were we having a baby shower. Just think our little ones will grow up together."

"I'm excited about that. You already have a yard full of "kids" but you need the human variety." Beth raised miniature goats—even had a calendar business featuring dressed-up goats.

"Tell me about it. My kids are really rambunctious right now. I was getting a calendar shoot set up two days ago and one of them head butted me when I wasn't looking. Of course, I landed in the dirt and instantly had five kids jumping up and down on my back. It scared Cooper to death and he's demanded that I stay out of the pen when he's not with me. I've agreed since with this growing belly I'm a little off balance." She patted her growing tummy. Lana and Cam's baby was due between Christmas and New Year's and theirs was due early March.

"I agree that's a good plan. I remember a few times growing up during county fair days when I was butted by a goat and ended up face down in the dirt beneath a herd of goats.

"Well, I love your little cutie-pie goats," Aunt Trudy harrumphed, "but I want a house full of nieces and nephews. You and Cooper have stepped up like Lana, but the other brothers need to get busy."

Beth laughed. "We can't wait, Aunt Trudy."

"We're holding off. For a few months anyway, as we enjoy a little us time," Jenna said, looking apologetic.

"I heard that," her aunt Sally Ann called from the kitchen. "I have the ears of an elephant where babies are concerned."

Jenna leaned toward the short hallway to the kitchen. "Don't worry, Aunt Trudy *and* Aunt Sally Ann—we're hoping to have a houseful."

"I'm ready when y'all are," Aunt Sally Ann called back and chuckled.

"Agreed," Aunt Trudy added.

Jenna was really busy getting her marketing consulting business set up. Lana completely understood her reasoning. But Lana hadn't wanted to wait. She and Cam had talked about it and after they'd married, she'd chosen to take off from teaching this year and fulfill both of their dreams of having a baby. She was happy, overjoyed, ecstatic…but deep inside there was that longing to share with her mother, and sometimes a deep sadness just overtook her as it had last night. But she wasn't going there today and pushed the longing deep into her heart and focused on the joy in the room. The joy of this time, and the knowledge that if her mother had been able to, she would have been here physically as much as she was in spirit.

Maisy jumped into the conversation and laid an arm across Aunt Trudy's shoulders. "Drake and I have to get married before we even think about babies. So you're out of luck on our end. I hope you still love me."

"Please keep loving me too." Libby grinned. "Me and Vance aren't ready, not this year anyway. I can't even imagine with our schedule."

"I will always love y'all. But you can't blame me for trying." Aunt Trudy's eyes twinkled and she swatted Maisy's hip. "I'm just getting impatient with all the excitement of getting one little baby soon, I'm wanting the whole lot of you to get busy."

A chorus of laughter and chatter ensued.

"Well," Sally Ann said as she came out from the kitchen. "If I can't have a baby from the rest of you, let's celebrate the one we are getting. Thank you very much, Lana and Beth. Let's get some delicious cake. Whoever finds the pink baby shoes inside their piece of cake gets a prize. So chew carefully," She sang the last word and everyone moved from the living room to the bright kitchen.

Lana rose from the deeply cushioned armchair and stretched her cramping back.

"Is your back hurting?" Libby asked as they walked toward the kitchen and the promise of cake. "You look a little tired. See, I can't be being tired out there trying to keep up with Vance's schedule."

"No, you don't need to be thinking about that just yet. My back is hurting some and my energy comes and goes. I can't stay in one position too long so standing up feels good."

"Maybe it'll help you. And thanks for agreeing with me. Aunt Trudy had me feeling a little guilty."

Lana chuckled. "You'll get used to people wanting to know when you're expecting. You'll learn to ignore any guilt. It's about you and Vance and when it's right for the two of you."

Since Libby had come to town and fell in love with Vance, they'd been busy going from rodeo to rodeo ever since they'd gotten married. They were going after his dream of winning the saddle bronc championship in the National Finals Rodeo as a team effort. Lana loved that.

"So, are you excited about the big trip to Vegas for the finals?"

Libby bit her lip and looked both excited and a little worried. "I am so excited for Vance. He's on fire right now but I'm also very glad Drake and Maisy are coming to watch him compete. I'll have someone to hang around with when he's practicing. The thought of being in Las Vegas with a lot of time on my hands is a little overwhelming."

"I'm glad Drake and Maisy will be there too. I wish we could be but..." She chuckled, rubbed her baby bump and smiled at Libby. "But it's just too close to the due date. I wouldn't want to have this baby somewhere between here and Vegas."

"That would be scary. It's killing me and Vance that there is a possibility you'll have the baby and we won't be here, but we'd never want to put you at risk. We told Drake and Maisy they didn't have to come, just in case you had Eva Marie early, but they insisted on coming. Plus, Maisy is supposed to be on that cooking show while she's in town. And they said you and Cam insisted they needed to be the family representing Vance's cheering squad. You're a really wonderful person."

Lana wrapped an arm around Libby's waist and hugged her. "I want to see him win. He has worked so hard and been so very dedicated. He deserves this. And I am so glad he has you by his side. My littlest big brother." They both smiled at her reference to Vance. "I worried about him and now he just seems so very content. It makes my heart happy."

Libby looked suddenly emotional. "I hope so, because he made all my dreams come true and I love him so much."

"And he feels the same about you."

The back door opened and seven-year-old April rushed inside, followed by her mom, Bella. She was married to Lana's cousin, Carson. She had become a really good friend.

"Aunt Lana," April called, her face lit up like the Fourth of July. "I'm so glad we got to come have a party with you for the baby. I got her a new dress. But Mom said I needed to keep it a secret until you open the presents."

"*April*," Bella cooed, a playful warning in her words. "You were supposed to keep it a secret." She shook her head and struggled not to laugh.

April's eyes widened and she clamped a hand over her mouth. "I didn't mean to. It just came out."

Lana laughed as she bent down to embrace the little darling. "That's okay. It'll still be a surprise when I pull it out of the bag. You can help me open all the gifts. How's that?"

April squealed with delight. "Yes, I'm good at opening presents."

"Yes, you are." Bella set the present on the gift

table before coming over and giving Lana a hug. She whispered, "You've made her day and helped us all out by giving her something to do. She's been talking about this nonstop all the way here from our ranch."

"She's the perfect little helper."

April sparkled under the praise of the women. The child's mother had chosen her career over raising her and it had been so hard on Carson worrying about his little girl growing up without a mother. Lana felt deep empathy for April and had been so happy when Bella had come into their lives. April needed a woman in her life. April needed someone to be a mother to her.

"Aunt Lana, look at the baby boots. *They're so cute.*" April held the adorable tiny booties out to her— pale pink with silky flowers and tiny pearls for centers.

"They're beautiful and Eva Marie is going to look like a little doll wearing them. Don't you think?"

April nodded. "Can I come see her when you bring her home?"

Lana set the booties on the chair arm and patted the spot beside her on the chair. April was seven now but still small for her age. Lana wrapped her arms around her and held her close, inhaling the sweet scent of her strawberry shampoo. Over her little head, she saw everyone watching with tender looks on their faces. They all cared about this sweet little girl, too, who had needed a mother as bad as Lana did when she was growing up. Thankfully, Carson had met Bella and everyone had gotten their wish.

"You can come stay with me for a few days after Eva Marie arrives and we'll both take care of our baby. She's going to need lots of love and I think you're just the person to help with that. Plus, she's going to want to know you. She will always look up to you like a big sister. You will be very important in her life."

April turned very serious. "And she will be very important in my life."

"I'm glad, darling. Because we already know just how sweet and kind you are."

She giggled. "I'm a stinker sometimes. Daddy says so, but he's usually teasing me."

"He likes to tease. I remember when we were all growing up, your daddy and your uncles teased me all the time. But you know what? Whenever I needed them, they came running and they always took up for me."

Sometimes too much. It was her brothers always in her business that had her leaving Texas and taking a teaching job in Windswept Bay, Florida. It had been the best move of her life because while getting away from her brothers, she'd met Cam. And wouldn't you know it, the man had a ranch in Texas only two hours away from her family ranch.

"They love you."

"They love you, too, and they'll always be there for you too. So, are you excited about Thanksgiving tomorrow?"

"Yes, Mom says that my new cousins will be there. I haven't seen them since Uncle Brice married Tara. I'm excited to get to play with Jed and Paige."

"It's going to be a fun day and I know they're looking forward to coming back from their grandparent's house so they can see you."

The kids had gotten along so well at the wedding. They were at Tara's parents today but would be back tomorrow in time for the big Thanksgiving town festival that was being held.

"It's going to be a fun day," Maisy said. "And I baked some cupcakes you'll have to try. And Libby baked pies last night."

"Eating is a great part of it." Gert grinned from where she was sorting gifts, getting them ready to pass out. "The funniest part is watching the cowboys compete against each other."

True. Everyone would be there and it looked like it was going to be a lot of fun as it would be one big potluck dinner and everyone was invited. Lana loved her little town.

"I'm just glad we got to be here for a few days," Libby said. "I can't wait to watch everyone do their thing."

"Me either," Maisy agreed. "I've never been to this one, but I love festivals and Drake said it was a blast."

"It sure is," Aunt Trudy said. "Cowboys everywhere, trying to impress their girls. You're all going to have fun tomorrow."

"Oh, it's going to be a big day." Sally Ann passed around a tray of cookies that looked like angels wearing pink halos. "Your daddy and all your uncles are frying turkeys and there'll be mountains and mountains of Thanksgiving dressing and cranberry sauce."

April's expression contorted into a look of horror at the mention of cranberry sauce. "Yuck. I'm not eating that purple stuff."

"You don't have to." Aunt Trudy reached for a cookie and took a nibble. "There will be plenty of things there you'll love. We're going to play games too. So, you and Jed and Paige will have fun with all the other kids."

That made April beam with delight. Lana was looking forward to the festival. As everyone talked about the festival April began opening the baby gifts again, Lana was able to nestle back in her chair and relax. The ache in her back that had been coming and going was coming back. A sharp pain suddenly stabbed through her lower back and she sucked in a tight breath then let it ease out as she tried to hide her discomfort.

A Braxton Hicks contraction? She tried hard to suck in short breaths without being conspicuous. It helped ease the pain. She'd known the false labor pains were predicted by her doctor to start in the last month; she decided not to mention them to anyone. Besides, Cam was already tightly wound, though he was trying hard not to let her see it. She could tell that her serious husband, so much like her oldest brother Drake, was taking his new daddy responsibilities to the next level. She was not going to say or do anything that would make him worry more. Him catching her in a weak moment last night thinking about her sweet mother had instantly etched his brow with concern.

Her checkup was in two days and she would ask her doctor about all the pains. It would be good for her peace of mind prior to catching the jet to Windswept Bay that Gage was sending for them. She'd tell the doctor about her pains just in case they weren't Braxton Hicks or something else…her thoughts went to her mother and the constant wonder about how she felt before she went to the hospital to have Lana and ended up dead.

Not a good place to go.

Beth handed April a package and she tore into it, paper flew everywhere. Lana fought to keep her spirits up and concentrated on the little girl as she threw herself into getting to the bottom of the package. There at last she pulled out an adorable frilly pink dress and a black and white polka dot dress just as sweet.

Lana felt her throat clog as a strange mixture of happiness and melancholy swirled through her at seeing the beautiful outfits. She could see her cherub-faced baby in the outfits and her heart yanked hard. She couldn't wait to meet her baby girl. If only she lived to see her.

She blinked away the threat of tears and forced all her efforts on the happy thoughts. She would see her baby soon. That glorious day was going to be here before she blinked twice.

Soon.

Soon she would get to do what her own mother never experienced: she would get to hold her baby girl in her arms. And in doing so, maybe it would ease the ache of what she'd missed all these years. Maybe in some way she could turn back time and experience that same gift for her mother.

If only…

More Books by Debra Clopton

Star Gazer Inn of Corpus Christi Bay
What New Beginnings are Made of (Book 1)
What Dreams are Made of (Book 2)
What Hopes are Made of (Book 3)
What a Heart's Desire is Made of (Book 4)
What True Love is Made of (Book 5)

Sunset Bay Romance
Longing for Forever (Book 1)
Longing for a Hero (Book 2)
Longing for Love (Book 3)
Longing for Ever After (Book 4)
Longing for You (Book 5)
Longing for Us (Book 6)

Texas Brides & Bachelors
Heart of a Cowboy (Book 1)
Trust of a Cowboy (Book 2)
True Love of a Cowboy (Book 3)

New Horizon Ranch Series
Her Texas Cowboy: Cliff (Book 1)
Rescued by Her Cowboy: Rafe (Book 2)
Protected by Her Cowboy: Chase (Book 3)
Loving Her Best Friend Cowboy: Ty (Book 4)
Family for a Cowboy: Dalton (Book 5)
The Mission of Her Cowboy: Treb (Book 6)
Maddie's Secret Baby (Book 7)
This Cowgirl Loves This Cowboy: Austin (Book 8)

Turner Creek Ranch Series
Treasure Me, Cowboy (Book 1)
Rescue Me, Cowboy (Book 2)
Complete Me, Cowboy (Book 3)
Sweet Talk Me, Cowboy (Book 4)

Cowboys of Ransom Creek
Her Cowboy Hero (Book 1)
The Cowboy's Bride for Hire (Book 2)
Cooper: Charmed by the Cowboy (Book 3)
Shane: The Cowboy's Junk-Store Princess (Book 4)
Vance: Her Second-Chance Cowboy (Book 5)
Drake: The Cowboy and Maisy Love (Book 6)
Brice: Not Quite Looking for a Family (Book 7)

Texas Matchmaker Series
Dream With Me, Cowboy (Book 1)
Be My Love, Cowboy (Book 2)
This Heart's Yours, Cowboy (Book 3)
Hold Me, Cowboy (Book 4)
Be Mine, Cowboy (Book 5)
Operation: Married by Christmas (Book 6)
Cherish Me, Cowboy (Book 7)
Surprise Me, Cowboy (Book 8)
Serenade Me, Cowboy (Book 9)
Return To Me, Cowboy (Book 10)
Love Me, Cowboy (Book 11)
Ride With Me, Cowboy (Book 12)
Dance With Me, Cowboy (Book 13)

Windswept Bay Series
From This Moment On (Book 1)
Somewhere With You (Book 2)
With This Kiss (Book 3)
Forever and For Always (Book 4)
Holding Out For Love (Book 5)
With This Ring (Book 6)
With This Promise (Book 7)
With This Pledge (Book 8)
With This Wish (Book 9)
With This Forever (Book 10)
With This Vow (Book 11)

About the Author

Bestselling author Debra Clopton has sold over 2.5 million books. Her book OPERATION: MARRIED BY CHRISTMAS has been optioned for an ABC Family Movie. Debra is known for her contemporary, western romances, Texas cowboys and feisty heroines. Sweet romance and humor are always intertwined to make readers smile. A sixth generation Texan she lives with her husband on a ranch deep in the heart of Texas. She loves being contacted by readers.

Visit Debra's website at www.debraclopton.com

Sign up for Debra's newsletter at www.debraclopton.com/contest/

Check out her Facebook at www.facebook.com/debra.clopton.5

Follow her on Twitter at @debraclopton

Contact her at debraclopton@ymail.com

If you enjoyed reading *With This Forever* I would appreciate it if you would help others enjoy this book, too.

Recommend it. Please help other readers find this book by recommending it to friends, reader's groups and discussion boards.

Review it. Please tell other readers why you liked this book by reviewing it on the retail site you purchased it from or Goodreads. If you do write a review, please send an email to debraclopton@ymail.com so I can thank you with a personal email. Or visit me at: www.debraclopton.com.

www.ingramcontent.com/pod-product-compliance
Lightning Source LLC
Chambersburg PA
CBHW071154180726
48291CB00007B/2455